George Colman

The Dramatick Works of George Colman

Volume 2

George Colman

The Dramatick Works of George Colman
Volume 2

ISBN/EAN: 9783337303372

Printed in Europe, USA, Canada, Australia, Japan

Cover: Foto ©Andreas Hilbeck / pixelio.de

More available books at **www.hansebooks.com**

THE

DRAMATICK WORKS

OF

GEORGE COLMAN.

VOLUME THE SECOND;

CONTAINING,

The ENGLISH MERCHANT, MAN and WIFE; Or,
The MAN of BUSINESS, The SHAKESPEARE JUBILEE.

———————————

LONDON,

Printed for T. BECKET, Adelphi, Strand.

MDCCLXXVII.

THE

ENGLISH MERCHANT.

A

COMEDY.

First acted at the Theatre-Royal in Drury-Lane, on the 21st of February, 1767.

Næ illiufmodi jam magna nobis civium
Penuria eft. Homo antiquâ virtute ac fide :
Haud cito mali quid ortum ex hoc fit publice.
Quam gaudeo, ubi etiam hujus generis reliquias
Reftare video ! TER.

TO

MONSIEUR DE VOLTAIRE

THE FOLLOWING COMEDY,

A TRIBUTE

DUE TO THE AUTHOR OF

L'ECOSSAISE,

IS INSCRIBED

BY HIS MOST OBEDIENT

HUMBLE SERVANT,

GEORGE COLMAN.

P R O L O G U E,

E A C H year how many Englifh vifit France,
'To learn the language, or to learn to dance!
'Twixt Dover-Cliffs and Calais, in July,
Obferve how thick the birds of paffage fly!
Fair-weather fops in fwarms, frefh-water failors,
Cooks, mantua-makers, milleners, and tailors!
Our bard too made a trip; and, fland'rers fay,
Brought home, among fome more run-goods, a play:
Here, on this quay, prepar'd t'unload his cargo,
If on the freight you lay not an embargo.
   " What! am I branded for a fmuggler?" cries
Out little Bayes, with anger in his eyes.
" No.   Englifh poets, Englifh Merchants made,
" To the whole world of letters fairly trade:
" With the rich ftores of ancient Rome and Greece,
" *Imported duty-free*, may fill their piece:
" Or, like Columbus, crofs th' Atlantick ocean,
" And fet Peru and Mexico in motion;
" Turn Cherokees and Catabaws to fhape;
" Or fail for *wit* and *humour* to the Cape."

Is

PROLOGUE.

Is there a *weaver* here from Spitalfields?
To his award our author fairly yields.
The *pattern*, he allows, is not quite new,
And he imports the *raw materials* too.
Come whence they will, from Lyons, Genoa, Rome,
'Tis Englifh filk when wrought in Englifh loom.
Silk! he recants; and owns, with lowly mind,
His manufacture is a coarfer kind.
Be it drab, drugget, flannel, doyley, friefe,
Rug, or whatever *winter-wear* you pleafe,
So it have leave to rank in any clafs,
Pronounce it *Englifh Stuff*, and let it pafs!

Dramatis

DRAMATIS PERSONÆ.

Lord FALBRIDGE,	*Mr. Powell.*
Sir WILLIAM DOUGLAS,	*Mr. Havard.*
FREEPORT,	*Mr. Yates.*
SPATTER,	*Mr. King.*
OWEN,	*Mr. Burton.*
LA FRANCE,	*Mr. Baddeley.*
OFFICER,	*Mr. Strange.*
Servants, &c.	
Lady ALTON,	*Mrs. Abington.*
AMELIA,	*Mrs. Palmer.*
Mrs. GOODMAN,	*Mrs. Hopkins.*
MOLLY,	*Miss Pope.*

SCENE, LONDON.

THE

ENGLISH MERCHANT.

ACT I.

SCENÉ, *a room in Mrs. Goodman's houfe.*

Enter Molly, ftruggling with Spatter.

Molly.

BE quiet, Mr. Spatter! let me alone! Pray now, Sir! It is a ftrange thing a body can't go about the houfe without being pefter'd with your impertinence. Why fure!

Spat. Introduce me to your miftrefs then—come, there's a good girl! and I will teaze you no longer.

Molly. Indeed I fha'n't. Introduce you to my lady! for what, pray?

Spat. Oh! for a thoufand things. To laugh, to chat, to take a difh of tea, to——

Molly. You drink tea with my lady! I fhould not have thought of that. On what acquaintance?

Spat.

Spat. The moſt agreeable in the world, child! a new acquaintance.

Molly. Indeed you miſtake yourſelf mightily: you are not a proper acquaintance for a perſon of her quality, I aſſure you, Sir!

Spat. Why, what quality is ſhe, then?

Molly. Much too high quality for your acquaintance, I promiſe you. What! a poet-man! that ſits, write, write, write, all day long, ſcribbling a pack of nonſenſe for the news-papers! You're fit for nothing above a chambermaid.

Spat. That's as much as to ſay, that you think me juſt fit for you. Eh, child?

Molly. No, indeed, not I, Sir. Neither my lady nor I will have any thing to ſay to you.

Spat. Your miſtreſs and you both give yourſelves a great many airs, my dear. Your poverty, I think, might pull down your pride.

Molly. What does the fellow mean by poverty?

Spat. I mean that you are ſtarving.

Molly. Oh, the ſlanderous monſter! we! ſtarving! who told you ſo? I'd have you to know, Sir, my lady has a very great fortune.

Spat. So 'tis a ſign, by her way of life and appearance.

Molly. Well; ſhe lives privately, indeed, becauſe
ſhe

she loves retirement; she goes plain, because she hates dress; she keeps no table, because she is an enemy to luxury. In short, my lady is as rich as a Jew, and you are an impertinent coxcomb.

Spat. Come, come! I know more of your mistress than you imagine.

Molly. And what do you know of her?

Spat. Oh, I know what I know.

Molly. Well!   [*Alarmed.*

Spat. I know who she is, and where she came from; I am very well acquainted with her family, and know her whole history.

Molly. How can that be?

Spat. Very easily—I have correspondence every where. As private as she may think herself, it is not the first 'time that I have seen or heard of Amelia.

Molly. Oh, gracious! as sure as I am alive this man will discover us. [*Apart.*] Mr. Spatter, my dear Mr. Spatter, if you know any thing, sure you would not be so cruel as to betray us!

Spat. My dear Mr. Spatter! O ho! I have guess'd right—there is something then.

Molly. No, Sir, there is nothing at all; nothing that signifies to you or any body else.

Spat. Well, well, I'll say nothing; but then you must——   *Molly.*

Molly. What?

Spat. Come; kifs me, hufly!

Molly. I fay kifs you, indeed!

Spat. And you'll introduce me to your miftrefs?

Molly. Not I, I promife you.

Spat. Nay, no myfteries between you and me, child! Come; here's the key to all locks, the clue to every maze, and the difclofer of all fecrets; money, child! Here! take this purfe; you fee I know fomething; tell me the reft, and I have the fellow to it in my pocket.

Molly. Ha, ha, ha! poor Mr. Spatter! Where could you get all this money, I wonder! Not by your poetries, I believe. But what fignifies telling you any thing, when you are acquainted with our whole hiftory already. You have correfpondence every where, you know. There, Sir! take up your filthy purfe again, and remember that I fcorn to be obliged to any body but my miftrefs.

Spat. There's impudence for you! when to my certain knowledge your miftrefs has not a guinea in the world; you live in continual fear of being difcovered; and you will both be utterly undone in a fortnight, unlefs lord Falbridge fhould prevent it, by taking Amelia under his protection. You underftand me, child.

Molly.

Molly. You fcandalous wretch! Did you ever hear fuch a monfter? I won't ftay a moment longer with him. But you are quite miftaken about me and my miftrefs, I affure you, Sir. We are in the beft circumftances in the world; we have nothing to fear; and we don't care a farthing for you.— So your fervant, Mr. Poet! [*Exit.*

Spatter alone.

Your fervant, Mrs. Pert! " We are in the beft " circumftances in the world." Ay, that is as much as to fay, they are in the utmoft diftrefs. " We have nothing to fear." That is, they are frightened out of their wits. " And we don't care " a farthing for you." Meaning, that they will take all the care in their power, that I fhall not find them out. But I may be too hard for you yet, young gentlewoman! I have earned but a poor livelihood by mere fcandal and abufe; but if I could once arrive at doing a little fubftantial mif-chief, I fhould make my fortune.

Enter Mrs. Goodman.

Oh! your fervant, Mrs. Goodman! Yours is the moft unfociable lodging-houfe in town. So many ladies, and only one gentleman! and you won't take the leaft notice of him.

Mrs.

Mrs. Good. How fo, Mr. Spatter?

Spat. Why, did not you promife to introduce me to Amelia?

Mrs. Good. To tell you the plain truth, Mr. Spatter, fhe don't like you. And, indeed, I don't know how it is, but you make yourfelf a great many enemies.

Spat. Yes; I believe I do raife a little envy.

Mrs. Good. Indeed you are miftaken, Sir. As you are a lodger of mine, it makes me quite uneafy to hear what the world fays of you. How do you contrive to make fo many enemies, Mr. Spatter?

Spat. Becaufe I have merit, Mrs. Goodman.

Mrs. Good. May be fo; but nobody will allow it but yourfelf. They fay that you fet up for a wit, indeed; but that you deal in nothing but fcandal, and think of nothing but mifchief.

Spat. I do fpeak ill of the men fometimes, to be fure; but then I have a great regard for women —provided they are handfome: and that I may give you a proof of it, introduce me to Amelia.

Mrs. Good. You muft excufe me; fhe and you would be the worft company in the world; for fhe never fpeaks too well of herfelf, nor the leaft ill of any body elfe. And then her virtue——

Spat. Pho, pho, fhe fpeaks ill of nobody, becaufe

caufe fhe knows nobody; and as for her virtue,
ha, ha!

Mrs. Good. You don't believe much in that, I
fuppofe?

Spat. I have not over-much faith, Mrs. Goodman. Lord Falbridge, perhaps, may give a better
account of it.

Mrs. Good. Lord Falbridge can fay nothing but
what would be extremely to her honour, I affure
you, Sir. [*Spatter laughs.*] Well, well, you may
laugh, but it is very true.

Spat. Oh, I don't doubt it; but you don't tell
the whole truth, Mrs. Goodman. When any of
your friends or acquaintance fit for their pictures,
you draw a very flattering likenefs. All characters
have their dark fide, and if they have but one eye,
you give them in *profile*. Your great friend, Mr.
Freeport, for inftance, whom you are always praif-
ing for his benevolent actions——

Mrs. Good. He is benevolence itfelf, Sir.

Spat. Yes, and groffnefs itfelf too. I remember
him thefe many years. He always cancels an obligation by the manner of conferring it; and does
you a favour, as if he were going to knock you
down.

Mrs. Good. A truce with your fatire, good Mr.
Spatter!

Spatter! Mr. Freeport is my beſt friend; I owe him every thing; and I can't endure the ſlighteſt reflection on his character. Beſides, *he* can have given no offence to lady Alton, whatever may be the caſe with Amelia.

Spat. Lady Alton! ſhe is a particular friend of mine to be ſure; but, between you and me, Mrs. Goodman, a more ridiculous character than any you have mentioned. A *bel eſprit* forſooth! and as vain of her beauty as learning, without any great portion of either. A fourth Grace, and a tenth Muſe! who fancies herſelf enamour'd of lord Falbridge, becauſe ſhe would be proud of ſuch a conqueſt; and has lately beſtowed ſome marks of diſtinction on me, becauſe ſhe thinks it will give her credit among perſons of letters.

Mrs. Good. Nay, if you can't ſpare your own friends, I don't wonder at your attacking mine— and ſo, Sir, your humble ſervant. But, ſtay! here's a poſt-chaiſe ſtopp'd at our door; and here comes a ſervant with a portmanteau! 'Tis the gentleman for whom my firſt floor was taken, I ſuppoſe.

Spat. Very likely; well, you will introduce me to him at leaſt, Mrs. Goodman.

Enter

Enter a servant with a portmanteau.   Sir William
Douglas following.

Sir Will. You are Mrs. Goodman, I suppose,
madam ?

Mrs. Good. At your service, Sir.

Sir Will. Mr. Owen, I believe, has secured apartments here ?

Mrs. Good. He has, Sir.

Sir Will. They are for me, madam. Have you
any other lodgers ?

Mrs. Good. Only that gentleman, Sir; and a
young lady——

Spat. Of great beauty and virtue. Eh, Mrs.
Goodman ?

Mrs. Good. She has both, Sir; but you will see
very little of her, for she lives in the most retired
manner in the world.

Sir Will. Her youth and beauty are matter of
great indifference to me; for I shall be as much a
recluse as herself.   Are there any news at present
stirring in London ?

Mrs. Good. Mr. Spatter can inform you, Sir, for
he deals in news.   In the mean while, I'll prepare
your apartments.   [*Exit, followed by the servant.*

Manent

Manent Sir William Douglas, and Spatter; Sir William walks up and down, without taking notice of Spatter.

Spat. This muſt be a man of quality by his ill manners. I'll ſpeak to him [*aſide.*] [*to Sir William.*] Will your lordſhip give me leave———

Sir Will. Lordſhip! I am no lord, Sir, and muſt beg not to be honoured with the name.

Spat. It is a kind of miſtake, that cannot diſ-pleaſe at leaſt.

Sir Will. I don't know that. None but a fool would be vain of a title, if he had one; and none but an impoſtor would aſſume a title, to which he has no right.

Spat. Oh, you're of the houſe of commons then, a member of parliament, and are come up to town to attend the ſeſſions, I ſuppoſe, Sir?

Sir Will. No matter what I am, Sir.

Spat. Nay, no offence, I hope, Sir. All I meant was to do you honour. Being concerned in two evening-poſts and one morning paper, I was wil-ling to know the proper manner of announcing your arrival.

Sir Will. You have connexions with the preſs then, it ſeems, Sir?

Spat. Yes, Sir; I am an humble retainer to the Muſes,

Mufes, an author. I compofe pamphlets on all fubjects, compile magazines, and do news-papers.

Sir Will. Do news-papers! What do you mean by that, Sir?

Spat. That is, Sir, I collect the articles of news from the other papers and make new ones for the poftfcript, tranflate the mails, write occafional letters from Cato and Theatricus, and give fictitious anfwers to fuppofed correfpondents.

Sir Will. A very ingenious as well as honourable employment, I muft confefs, Sir.

Spat. Some little genius is requifite, to be fure. Now, Sir, if I can be of any ufe to you—if you have any friend to be praifed, or any enemy to be abufed; any author to cry up, or minifter to run down; my pen and talents are entirely at your fervice.

Sir Will. I am much obliged to you, Sir, but at prefent I have not the leaft occafion for either. In return for your genteel offers, give me leave to trouble you with one piece of advice. When you deal in private fcandal, have a care of the cudgel; and when you meddle with publick matters, beware of the pillory!

Spat. How, Sir! are you no friend to literature? Are you an enemy to the liberty of the prefs?

Sir Will. I have the greatest respect for both; but railing is the disgrace of letters, and personal abuse the scandal of freedom: Foul-mouthed criticks, are in general disappointed authors; and they, who are the loudest against ministers, only mean to be paid for their silence.

Spat. They may be sometimes, Sir; but give me leave to ask you——

Sir Will. Do not ask me at present, Sir! I see a particular friend of mine coming this way, and I must beg you to withdraw.

Spat. Withdraw, Sir? first of all allow me to—

Sir Will. Nay, no reply! we must be in private.   [*thrusting out Spatter.*

Sir William Douglas alone.

What a wretch! as contemptible as mischievous. Our generous mastiffs fly at men from an instinct of courage; but this fellow's attacks proceed from an instinct of baseness.—But here comes the faithful Owen, with as many good qualities as that execrable fellow seems to have bad ones.

Enter Owen.

Well, Owen; I am safe arrived you see.

Owen. Ah, Sir! would to Heaven you were as safe returned again! Have a care of betraying
                                                        yourself

yourfelf to be Sir William Douglas!—During
your ftay here, your name is Ford, remember.

Sir Will. I fhall take care. But tell me your
news! What have you done fince your arrival?
Have you heard any thing of my daughter? Have
you feen lord Brumpton? Has he any hope of
obtaining my pardon?

Owen. He had, Sir.

Sir Will. And what can have deftroyed it then?

Owen. My lord Brumpton is dead, Sir.

Sir Will. Dead!

Owen. I faw him within this week in apparent
good health; he promifed to exert his whole intereft in your favour: By his own appointment I
went to wait on him yefterday noon, when I was
ftunned with the news of his having died fuddenly
the evening before.

Sir Will. My lord Brumpton dead! the only
friend I had remaining in England; the only perfon, on whofe interceffion I relied for my pardon.
Cruel fortune! I have now no hope, but to find
my daughter. Tell me, Owen; have you been
able to hear any tidings of her?

Owen. Alas, Sir, none that are fatisfactory.
On the death of Mr. Andrews, in whofe care you
left her, being cruelly abandoned by the relation

who

who fucceeded to the eftate, fhe left the country fome months ago, and has not fince been heard of.

Sir Will. Unhappy there too! When will the meafure of my misfortunes be full? When will the malice of my fate be fatisfied? Profcribed, condemned, attainted, (alas, but too juftly!) I have loft my rank, my eftate, my wife, my fon, and all my family. One only daughter remains. Perhaps a wretched wanderer like myfelf, perhaps in the extremeft indigence, perhaps difhonoured— Ha! that thought diftracts me.

Owen. My dear mafter, have patience! Do not be ingenious to torment yourfelf, but confult your fafety, and prepare for your departure.

Sir Will. No, Owen. Hearing, providentially, of the death of my friend Andrews, paternal care and tendernefs drew me hither; and I will not quit the kingdom till I learn fomething of my child, my dear Amelia, whom I left a tender innocent in the arms of the beft of women twenty years ago. Her fex demands protection; and fhe is now of an age, in which fhe is more expofed to misfortunes than even in helplefs infancy.

Owen. Be advifed; depart, and leave that care to me. Confider, your life is now at ftake.

Sir Will. My life has been too miferable to

render

render me very folicitous for its prefervation.—But the complection of the times is changed; the very name of the party, in which I was unhappily engaged, is extinguifhed, and the whole nation is unanimoufly devoted to the throne. Difloyalty and infurrection are now no more, and the fword of juftice is fuffered to fleep. If I can find my child, and find her worthy of me, I will fly with her to take refuge in fome foreign country; if I am difcovered in the fearch, I have ftill fome hopes of mercy.

Owen. Heaven grant your hopes may be well founded!

Sir Will. Come, Owen! let us behave at leaft with fortitude in our adverfity! Follow me to my apartment, and let us confult what meafures we fhall take in fearching for Amelia. [*Exeunt.*

Scene changes to *Amelia's apartment.*

Amelia and Molly.

Amelia. Poor Molly! to be teazed with that odious fellow, Spatter!

Molly. But, madam, Mr. Spatter fays he is acquainted with your whole hiftory.

Amelia. Mere pretence, in order to render himfelf formidable. Be on your guard againft him, my

dear

dear Molly; and remember to conceal my mifery from him and all the world. I can bear poverty, but am not proof againft infult and contempt.

Molly. Ah, my dear miftrefs, it is to no purpofe to endeavour to hide it from the world. They will fee poverty in my looks. As for you, you can live upon the air; the greatnefs of your foul feems to fupport you; but lack-a-day, I fhall grow thinner and thinner every day of my life.

Amelia. I can fupport my own diftrefs, but yours touches me to the foul. Poor Molly! the labour of my hands fhall feed and clothe you. Here! difpofe of this embroidery to the beft advantage; what was formerly my amufement, muft now become the means of our fubfiftence. Let us be obliged to nobody, but owe our fupport to induftry and virtue.

Molly. You're an angel: Let me kifs thofe dear hands that have worked this precious embroidery; let me bathe them with my tears! You're an angel upon earth. I had rather ftarve in your fervice, than live with a princefs. What can I do to comfort you?

Amelia. Thou faithful creature! only continue to be fecret: You know my real character; you know I am in the utmoft diftrefs; I have opened

my

my heart to you; but you will plant a dagger there, if you betray me to the world.

Molly. Ah, my dear miſtreſs, how ſhould I betray you? I go no where, I converſe with nobody, but yourſelf and Mrs. Goodman: Beſides, the world is very indifferent about other peoples' misfortunes.

Amelia. The world is indifferent, it is true; but it is curious, and takes a cruel pleaſure in tearing open the wounds of the unfortunate.

Enter Mrs. Goodman.

Mrs. Goodman!

Mrs. Good. Excuſe me, madam: I took the liberty of waiting on you to receive your commands. 'Tis now near three o'clock. You have provided nothing for dinner, and have ſcarce taken any refreſhment theſe three days.

Amelia. I have been indiſpoſed.

Mrs. Good. I am afraid you are more than indiſpoſed—You are unhappy—Pardon me! but I cannot help thinking that your fortune is unequal to your appearance.

Amelia. Why ſhould you think ſo? You never heard me complain of my fortune.

Mrs. Good. No, but I have too much reaſon to believe it is inferior to your merit,

Amelia.

Amelia. Indeed, you flatter me.

Mrs. Good. Come, come ; you muſt not indulge this melancholy. I have a new lodger, an elderly gentleman, juſt arrived, who does me the honour to partake of my dinner; and I muſt have your company too. He ſeems to be in trouble as well as you. You muſt meet ; two perſons in affliction may perhaps become a conſolation to each other. Come, let us take ſome care of you !

Amelia. Be aſſured, Mrs. Goodman, I am much obliged to you for your attention to me ; but I want nothing.

Mrs. Good. Dear madam ! you ſay you want nothing, and you are in want of every thing.

Enter Servant.

Serv. [*to Mrs. Good.*] Lady Alton, madam, ſends her compliments, and will wait upon you after dinner.

Mrs. Good. Very well ; my beſt reſpects to her ladyſhip, and I ſhall be ready to attend her. [*Exit Servant.*] There, there is one cauſe of your uneaſineſs ! Lady Alton's viſit is on your account. She thinks you have robbed her of Lord Falbridge's affections, and that is the occaſion of her honouring me with her company.

Amelia. Lord Falbridge's affections !

Mrs,

Mrs. Good. Ah, my dear Amelia, you don't know your power over his heart. You have reconciled it to virtue. But, come! let me prevail on you to come with me to dinner.

Amelia. You muſt excuſe me.

Mrs. Good. Well, well, then I'll ſend you ſomething to your own apartment. If you have any other commands, pray honour me with them; for I would fain oblige you, if I knew how it were in my power. [*Exit.*

Manent Amelia and Molly.

Amelia. What an amiable woman! If it had not been for her apparent benevolence and goodneſs of heart, I ſhould have left the houſe on Mr. Spatter's coming to lodge in it.

Molly. Lady Alton, it ſeems, recommended him as a lodger here; ſo he can be no friend of yours on that account; for to be ſure ſhe owes you no good will, on account of my lord Falbridge.

Amelia. No more of lord Falbridge, I beſeech you, Molly. How can you perſiſt in mentioning him, when you know that, preſuming on my ſituation, he has dared to affront me with diſhonourable propoſals?

Molly. Ah, madam! but he ſorely repents it, I promiſe you, and would give his whole eſtate for

an

an opportunity of feeing you once more, and getting into your good graces again.

Amelia. No ; his ungenerous conduct has thrown him as much below me, as my condition had placed me beneath him. He imagined he had a right to infult my diftrefs ; but I will teach him to think it refpectable. [*Exeunt.*

A C T II,

SCENE, *An apartment at Mrs. Goodman's.*

Enter lady Alton and Spatter.

Spat. BUT you won't hear me, madam!

L. Alt. I have heard too much, Sir, This wandering *incognita* a woman of virtue ! I have no patience.

Spat. Mrs. Goodman pretends to be convinced of her being a perfon of honour.

L. Alt. A perfon of honour, and openly receive vifits from men ! feduce lord Falbridge ! No, no : Referve this character for your next novel, Mr. Spatter ! it is an affront to my underftanding. I begin to fufpect you have betrayed me ; you have

gone

gone over to the adverfe party, and are in the confpiracy to abufe me.

Spat. I, madam! Neither her beauty, nor her virtue——

L. Alt. Her beauty! her virtue! Why, thou wretch, thou grub of literature! whom I, as a patronefs of learning and encourager of men of letters, willing to blow the dead coal of genius, fondly took under my protection, do you remember what I have done for you?

Spat. With the utmoft gratitude, madam.

L. Alt. Did not I draw you out of the garret, where you daily fpun out your flimfy brain to catch the town flies in your cobweb diſſertations? Did not I introduce you to lord Dapperwit, the Apollo of the age? And did not you dedicate your filly volume of Poems on Several Occaſions to him? Did not I put you into the lift of my viſitors, and order my porter to admit you at dinner-time? Did not I write the only ſcene in your execrable farce, which the audience vouchfafed an hearing? And did not my female friend, Mrs. Melpomene, furnifh you with Greek and Latin mottoes for your twopenny eſſays?

Spat. I acknowledge all your ladyfhip's goodnefs to me. I have done every thing in my power to fhew my gratitude, and fulfil your ladyfhip's commands.

L. Alt.

L. Alt. Words, words, Mr. Spatter! You have been witnefs of lord Falbridge's inconftancy. A perfidious man! falfe as Phaon to Sappho, or Jafon to Medea! You have feen him defert me for a wretched vagabond; you have feen me abandoned like Calypfo, without making a fingle effort to recall my faithlefs Ulyffes from the Siren that has lured him from me.

Spat. Be calm but one moment, madam, and I'll——

L. Alt. Bid the fea be calm, when the winds are let loofe upon it. I have reafon to be enraged. I placed you in genteel apartments in this houfe, merely to plant you as a fpy; and what have you done for me? Have you employed your correfpondence to any purpofe? or difcovered the real character of this infamous woman, this infolent Amelia?

Spat. I have taken every poffible method to detect her. I have watched Amelia herfelf like a bailiff, or a duenna; I have overheard private converfations; have founded the landlady; tampered with the fervants; opened letters; and intercepted meffages.

L. Alt. Good creature! my beft Spatter! And what? what have you difcovered?

Spat. That Amelia is a native of Scotland; that
her

her furname *Walton* is probably not real, but af-
fumed; and that fhe earneftly wifhes to conceal
both the place of her birth and her family. -

L. Alt. And is that all?

Spat. All that I have been able to learn as yet,
madam.

L. Alt. Wretch! of what fervice have you been
then? Are thefe your boafted talents? When we
want to unravel an ambiguous character, you have
made out that fhe wifhes to lie concealed; and
when we wifh to know who fhe is, you have juft
difcovered that fhe is a native of Scotland.

Spat. And yet, if you will give me leave, madam, I think I could convince you that thefe difcoveries, blind and unfatisfactory as they may appear to you at firft, are of no fmall confequence.

L. Alt. Of what confequence can they poffibly
be to me, man?

Spat. I'll tell you, madam. It is a rule in politicks, when we difcover fomething to add fomething more. Something added to fomething, makes
a good deal; upon this bafis I have formed a fyllogifm.

L. Alt. What does the pedant mean? A fyllogifm!

Spat. Yes, a fyllogifm; as for example: Any
perfon

perfon who is a native of Scotland, and wifhes to be concealed, muft be an enemy to the government. Amelia is a native of Scotland, and wifhes to be concealed. *Ergo*, Amelia is an enemy to the government.

L. Alt. Excellent! admirable logick! but I wifh we could prove it to be truth.

Spat. I would not lay a wager of the truth of it; but I would fwear it.

L. Alt. What, on a proper occafion, and in a proper place, my good Spatter?

Spat. Willingly; we muft make ufe of what we know, and even of what we don't know. Truth is of a dry and fimple nature, and ftands in need of fome little ornament. A lie, indeed, is infamous; but fiction, your ladyfhip, who deals in poetry, knows is beautiful.

L. Alt. But the fubftance of your fiction, Spatter?

Spat. I will lodge an information that the father of Amelia is a difaffected perfon, and has fent her to London for treafonable purpofes; nay, I can upon occafion even fuppofe the father himfelf to be in London: In confequence of which you will probably recover lord Falbridge, and Amelia will be committed to prifon.

L. Alt.

L. Alt. You have given me new life. I took you for a mere ftainer of paper; but I have found you a Machiavel.—I hear fomebody coming.—Mrs. Goodman has undertaken to fend Amelia hither. Ha! fhe's here! Away, Spatter, and wait for me at my houfe: You muft dine with me; and after dinner, like true politicians, we will fettle our plan of operations over our coffee. Away, away, this inftant! [*Exit Spatter.*

Lady Alton alone.

A convenient engine this Mr. Spatter: The moft impudent thorough-paced knave in the three kingdoms! with the heart of Zoilus, the pen of Mævius, and the tongue of Therfites. I was fure he would ftick at nothing. The writings of authors are publick advertifements of their qualifications; and when they profefs to live upon fcandal, it is as much as to fay, that they are ready for every other dirty work, in which we chufe to employ them. But now for Amelia! If fhe proves tractable, I may forego the ufe of this villain, who almoft makes me hate my triumph, and be afhamed of my revenge.

Enter Amelia.

Amelia. Mrs. Goodman has informed me that your ladyfhip has defired to fee me: I wait your commands, madam.

L. Alt.

L. Alt. Look you, young woman: I am fenfible how much it is beneath a perfon of my rank, to parley with one of your condition. For once, however, I am content to wave all ceremony; and if you behave as you ought to do, you have nothing to fear, child.

Amelia. I hope I have never behaved otherwife than as I ought to do, madam.

L. Alt. Yes; you have received the vifits of lord Falbridge; you have endeavoured to eftrange his affections from me: But, if you encourage him in his infidelity to me, tremble for the confequence! Be advifed, or you are ruined.

Amelia. I am confcious of no guilt, and know no fear, madam.

L. Alt. Come, come, Mrs. Amelia, this high ftrain is out of character with me. Act over your Clelia, and Cleopatra, and Caffandra, at a proper time; and let me talk in the ftile of nature and common fenfe to you. You have no lord Falbridge, no weak young nobleman, to impofe upon at prefent.

Amelia. To impofe upon! I fcorn the imputation, and am forry to find that your ladyfhip came hither, merely to indulge yourfelf in the cruel pleafure of infulting one of the unhappieft of her fex.   [*Weeping.*
                                            L. Alt.

L. Alt. You are miftaken; I came hither to con-
cert meafures for your happinefs, to affift your
poverty, and relieve your diftrefs. Leave this
houfe ; leave London ; I will provide you a retirement in the country, and fupply all your wants.
Only renounce all thoughts of lord Falbridge,
and never let him know the place of your retreat.

Amelia. Lord Falbridge! what is lord Falbridge
to me, madam ?

L. Alt. To convince me you have no commerce
with him, accept of my propofals.

Amelia. No, madam ; the favours which you intend me, I could not receive without blufhing. I
have no wants but what I can fupply myfelf; no
diftreffes which your ladyfhip can relieve ; and I
will feek no refuge but in my own virtue.

L. Alt. Your virtue! Ridiculous! If you are
a woman of virtue, what is the meaning of all
this myftery ? Who are you ? what are you ? who
will vouch for your character ?

Amelia. It wants no vouchers ; nor will I fuffer
myfelf to be arraigned like a criminal, till I know
by what authority you take upon you to act as my
judge.

L. Alt. Matchlefs confidence! Yes, yes, it is
too plain ! I fee you are the very creature I took

you for ; a mere adventurer ! Some ſtrolling prin-
ceſs, that are perhaps more frugal of your favours
than the reſt of your ſiſterhood, merely to enhance
the price of them.

Amelia. Hold, madam ! This opprobrious language is more injurious to your own honour than
to mine.   I ſee the violence of your temper, and
will leave you.   But you may one day know that
my birth is equal to your own ; my heart is perhaps more generous ; and whatever may be my
ſituation, I ſcorn to be dependant on any body ;
much leſs on one, who has ſo mean an opinion of
me, and who conſiders me as her rival.   [*Exit.*

Lady Alton alone.

Her rival ! Unparalleled inſolence ! An open
avowal of her competition with me ! Yes ; I ſee
Spatter muſt be employed.   Her rival ! I ſhall
burſt with indignation !

Enter Mrs. Goodman.

L. Alt. Mrs. Goodman ! where is Mr. Spatter ?

Mrs. Good. He went out the moment he left
your ladyſhip.   But you ſeem diſordered ; ſhall I
get you ſome hartſhorn, madam ?

L. Alt. Some poiſon.—Rival ! I ſhall choke with
rage.—You ſhall hear from me.   You, and your
Amelia.

Amelia. You have abufed me; you have con-
fpired againft my peace; and be affured you fhall
fuffer for it!   [*Exit.*

Mrs. Goodman alone.

What a violent woman! Her paffion makes her
forget what is due to her fex and quality. Ha!
Mr. Freeport!

Enter Freeport.

My beft friend! welcome to London! When did
you arrive from Lifbon?

Free. But laft night.

Mrs. Good. I hope you have had a pleafant
voyage?

Free. A good trading voyage—I have got money, but I have got the fpleen too.—Have you
any news in town?

Mrs. Good. None at all, Sir.

Free. So much the better. The lefs news, the
lefs nonfenfe.—But what ftrange lady have you
had here? I met her as I was coming up: She
rufhed by like a fury, and almoft fwept me down
ftairs again with the wind of her hoop-petticoat.

Mrs. Good. Ah! Jealoufy! Jealoufy is a terri-
ble paffion; efpecially in a woman's breaft, Mr.
Freeport.

Free.

Free. Jealoufy! Why, fhe is not jealous of you, Mrs. Goodman?

Mrs. Good. No; but of a lodger of mine.

Free. Have you any new lodgers fince I left you?

Mrs. Good. Two or three, Sir; the laft arrived but to-day; an elderly gentleman, who will fee no company.

Free. He's in the right. Three parts in four of mankind are knaves or fools; and the fourth part live by themfelves.—But who are your other lodgers?

Mrs. Good. An author, and a lady.

Free. I hate authors. Who is the lady?

Mrs. Good. She calls herfelf Amelia Walton; but I believe that name is not her real one.

Free. Not her real one! Why, fure fhe is a wo-man of charaƈter?

Mrs. Good. A woman of charaƈter! She is an angel. She is moft miferably poor; and yet haughty to an excefs.

Free. Pride and poverty! A fad compofition, Mrs. Goodman.

Mrs. Good. No, Sir; her pride is one of her greateft virtues: It confifts in depriving herfelf of almoft all neceffaries, and concealing it from the world. Though every aƈtion fpeaks her to be a

woman

woman of birth and education, she lives upon the work of her own hands, without murmur or complaint. I make use of a thousand stratagems to assist her, against her will; I prevail on her to keep the money due for rent for her support, and furnish her with every thing she wants at half its prime cost; but if she perceives or suspects these little artifices, she takes it almost as ill as if I had attempted to defraud her. In short, Sir, her unshaken virtue and greatness of soul under misfortunes, make me consider her as a prodigy, and often draw tears of pity and admiration from me.

Free. Ah! womens' tears lie very near their eyes. I never cried in my life; and yet I can feel too; I can admire, I can esteem, but what signifies whimpering? Hark ye, Mrs. Goodman! This is a very extraordinary account you give of this young woman; you have raised my curiosity, and I'll go and see this lodger of yours; I am rather out of spirits, and it will serve to amuse me.

Mrs. Good. Oh, Sir, you can't see her; she neither pays visits nor receives them, but lives in the most retired manner in the world.

Free. So much the better. I love retirement as well as she. Where are her apartments?

Mrs.

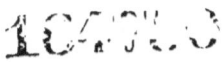

Mrs. Good. On this very floor, on the other fide of the ftaircafe.

Free. I'll go and fee her immediately.

Mrs. Good. Indeed you can't, Sir. It is impoffible.

Free. Impoffible! where is the impoffibility of going into a room? Come along!

Mrs. Good. For Heaven's fake, Mr. Freeport!

Free. Pfhaw! I have no time to lofe; I have bufinefs half an hour hence.

Mrs. Good. But won't it be rather indelicate, Sir? Let me prepare her firft!

Free. Prepare her? With all my heart. But remember that I am a man of bufinefs, Mrs. Goodman, and have no time to wafte in ceremony and compliment.   [*Exeunt.*

Amelia's apartment.

Amelia at work, and Molly.

Amelia. No, Polly! If lord Falbridge comes again, I am refolved not to fee him.

Molly. Indeed, madam, he loves you above all the world; I am fure of it; and I verily believe he will run mad, if you don't hear what he has to fay for himfelf.

Amelia. Speak no more of him.

Enter

Enter Mrs. Goodman.

Mrs. Goodman!

Mrs. Good. Pardon me, madam! here is a gentleman of my acquaintance begs you would give him leave to fpeak with you.

Amelia. A gentleman! who is he?

Mrs. Good. His name is Freeport, Madam. He has a few particularities; but he is the beft-hearted man in the world. Pray let him come in, madam!

Amelia. By no means; you know I receive vifits from nobody.

Enter Freeport.

Blefs me! he's here. This is very extraordinary, indeed, Mrs. Goodman.

Free. Don't difturb yourfelf, young woman; don't difturb yourfelf!

Molly. Mighty free and eafy, methinks!

Amelia. Excufe me, Sir; I am not ufed to receive vifits from perfons entirely unknown.

Free. Unknown! There is not a man in all London better known than I am. I am a merchant, my name is Freeport; Freeport of Crutched-Friars: enquire upon 'Change!

Amelia. Mrs. Goodman! I never faw the gentle-man before. I am furprifed at his coming here.

Free.

Free. Pho, prithee!—Mrs. Goodman knows me well enough. [*Mrs. Goodman talks apart with Amelia.*] Ay! that's right, Mrs. Goodman. Let her know who I am, and tell her to make herſelf eaſy.

Mrs. Good. But the lady does not chuſe we ſhould trouble her, Sir.

Free. Trouble her? I'll give her no trouble; I came to drink a diſh of tea with you; let your maid get it ready, and we will have it here inſtead of your parlour. In the mean time I will talk with this lady; I have ſomething to ſay to her.

Amelia. If you had any buſineſs, Sir——

Free. Buſineſs! I tell you I have very particular buſineſs; ſo ſit down, and let's have the tea.

Mrs. Good. You ſhould not have followed me ſo ſoon, Sir.

Free. Pho, prithee! [*Exit Mrs. Goodman.*

Molly. This is the oddeſt man I ever ſaw in my life.

Amelia. Well, Sir, as I ſee you are a particular acquaintance of Mrs. Goodman—But pray what are your commands for me, Sir? [*They ſit.*

Free. I tell you what, young woman; I am a plain man, and will tell you my mind in an inſtant. I am told that you are one of the beſt women in the

the world; very virtuous, and very poor; I like you for that: But they fay you are exceffively proud too; now I don't like you for that, madam.

Molly. Free and eafy ftill, I fee.

Amelia. And pray, Sir, who told you fo?

Free. Mrs. Goodman.

Amelia. She has deceived you, Sir; not in regard to my pride, perhaps, for there is a certain right pride which every body, efpecially women, ought to poffefs; and as to virtue, it is no more than my duty: But as to poverty, I difclaim it; they who want nothing, cannot be faid to be poor.

Free. It is no fuch thing: You don't fpeak the truth; and that is worfe than being proud. I know very well that you are as poor as Job, that you are in want of common neceffaries, and don't make a good meal above once in a fortnight.

Molly. My miftrefs fafts for her health, Sir.

Free. Hold your tongue, huffy! What, are you proud too?

Molly. Lord, what a ftrange man!

Free. But however, madam, proud or not proud, does not fignify twopence. Hark ye, young woman, it is a rule with me (as it ought to be with every good Chriftian) to give a tenth part of my fortune in charity. In the account of my profits,

there

there ftands at prefent the fum of two thoufand
pounds on the credit fide of my books; fo that I
am two hundred pounds in arrear. This I look
upon as a debt due from my fortune to your
poverty. Yes, your poverty, I fay, fo never deny
it. There's a bank-note for two hundred pounds;
and now I am out of your debt. Where the deuce
is this tea, I wonder?

Molly. I never faw fuch a man in my life.

Amelia. I don't know that I ever was fo thoroughly confounded. [*Apart.*]—Sir! [*To Freeport.*

Free. Well?

Amelia. This noble action has furprifed me ftill
more than your converfation, but you muft excufe
my refufal of your kindnefs; for I muft confefs,
that if I were to accept what you offer, I don't
know when I fhould be able to reftore it.

Free. Reftore it! why, who wants you to reftore
it? I never dreamt of reftitution.

Amelia. I feel, I feel your goodnefs to the bottom
of my foul; but you muft excufe me. I have no
occafion for your bounty; take your note, Sir, and
beftow it where it is wanted.

Molly. Lord, madam! you are ten times ftranger
than the gentleman. I tell you what, Sir; [*to
Freeport*] it does not figuify talking; we are in the
greateft

greateſt diſtreſs in the world, and if it had not been for the kindneſs and good-nature of Mrs. Goodman, we might have died by this time. My lady has concealed her diſtreſs from every body that was willing and able to relieve her; you have come to the knowledge of it in ſpite of her teeth; and I hope that you will oblige her, in ſpite of her teeth, to accept of your generous offer.

Amelia. No more, my dear Polly; if you would not have me die with ſhame, ſay no more! Return the gentleman his note, with my beſt thanks for his kindneſs; tell him, I durſt not accept of it; for when a woman receives preſents from a man, the world will always ſuſpect that ſhe pays for them at the expence of her virtue.

Free. What's that? what does ſhe ſay, child?

Molly. Lord, Sir, I hardly know what ſhe ſays. She ſays, that when a gentleman makes a young lady preſents, he is always ſuppoſed to have a deſign upon her virtue.

Free. Nonſenſe! why ſhould ſhe ſuſpect me of an ungenerous deſign, becauſe I do a generous action?

Molly. Do you hear, madam?

Amelia. Yes, I hear; I admire; but I muſt perſiſt in my refuſal: If that ſcandalous fellow Spatter

were

were to hear of this, he would ftick at faying nothing.

Free. Eh! what's that?

Molly. She is afraid you fhould be taken for her
lover, Sir.

Free. I for your lover! not I. ' I never faw you
before. I don't love you; fo make no fcruples
upon that account; I like you well enough, but I
don't love you at all; not at all, I tell you. If
you have a mind never to fee my face any more,
good bye t'ye! you fhall never fee me any more;
if you like I fhould come back again, I'll come
back again. But I lofc time; I have bufinefs; your
fervant! [*Going.*

Amelia. Stay, Sir! do not leave me without receiving the fincereft acknowledgments of my gratitude and efteem; but, above all, receive your
note again, and do not put me any longer to the
blufh!

Free. The woman is a fool!

Enter Mrs. Goodman.

Amelia. Come hither, I befeech you, Mrs. Goodman.

Mrs. Good. Your pleafure, madam!

Amelia. Here! take this note, which that gentleman

man has given me by miftake; return it to him, I
charge you! affure him of my efteem and admiration; but let him know I need no affiftance, and
cannot accept it.   [*Exit.*

Manent Freeport, &c.

Mrs. Good. Ah! Mr. Freeport! you have been
at your old trade. You are always endeavouring
to do good actions in fecret; but the world always
finds you out, you fee.

Molly. Well, I don't believe there are two
ftranger people in England than my miftrefs, and
that gentleman; one fo ready to part with money;
and the other fo unwilling to receive it. But don't
believe her, Sir; for, between friends, fhe is in
very great need of affiftance, I affure you.

Mrs. Good. Indeed I believe fo.

Free. Oh, I have no doubt on't; fo I'll tell you
what, Mrs. Goodman; keep the note, and fupply
her wants out of it without her knowledge; and,
now I think of it, that way is better than t'other.

Molly. I never faw fuch a ftrange man in my
life.   [*Exit.*

Mrs. Good. I fhall obey your kind commands,
Sir. Poor foul! my heart bleeds for her; her
virtue and misfortunes touch me to the foul.

Free.

Free. I have fome little feeling for her too; but ſhe is too proud. A fine face; fine figure; well behaved; well bred; and I dare ſay an excellent heart!—But ſhe is too proud; tell her ſo, d'ye hear? tell her ſhe is too proud. I ſhall be too late for my buſineſs—I'll ſee her again ſoon—It is a pity ſhe is ſo proud. [*Exeunt.*

A C T III.

Scene, a hall.

Sir William Douglas alone.

A YOUNG woman! a native of Scotland! her name Amelia! ſuppoſed to be in the greateſt diſtreſs, and living in total retirement! If fortune ſhould for once ſmile upon me, and have thrown me into the very ſame houſe! I don't know what to think of it; and yet ſo many un-common circumſtances together recall the memory of my misfortunes, and awaken all the father in my boſom.—I muſt be ſatisfied.

Enter Molly, croſſing the ſtage.

Sir Will. Madam! will you permit me to ſpeak one word to you ?

Molly.

Molly. [*coming forward.*] If you pleafe. What is your pleafure, Sir?

Sir Will. I prefume, Madam, you are the charming young woman I heard of?

Molly. I have a few charms in the eyes of fome folks, to be fure, Sir.

Sir Will. And you are a native of Scotland, they tell me?

Molly. I am, at your fervice, Sir.

Sir Will. Will you give me leave to afk the name of your family? Who is your father?

Molly. I really don't remember my father.

Sir Will. Ha! not remember him, do you fay?
                                    [*Earneftly.*

Molly. No, Sir; but I have been told that he was——

Sir Will. Who, madam?

Molly. One of the moft eminent bakers in Aberdeen, Sir.

Sir Will. Oh, I conceive! You live, I fuppofe, with the young lady I meant to fpeak to. I miftook you for the lady herfelf.

Molly. You did me a great deal of honour, I affure you, Sir.

Sir Will. But you are acquainted with your miftrefs's family?

                                    Molly.

Molly. Family, Sir!

Sir Will. Ay; who are her parents?

Molly. She comes of very creditable parents, I promife you, Sir.

Sir Will. I don't doubt it; but who are they? I have particular reafons for enquiring.

Molly. Very likely fo; but I muft beg to be excufed, Sir.

Sir Will. Of what age is your miftrefs? You will tell me that at leaft.

Molly. Oh, as to her age, fhe don't care who knows that; fhe is too young to deny her age yet a-while. She is about one-and-twenty, Sir.

Sir Will. Precifely the age of my Amelia! [*apart.* One-and-twenty, you fay?

Molly. Yes, Sir; and I am about two-and-twenty; there is no great difference between us.

Sir Will. [*apart.*] It muft be fo; her age, her country, her manner of living, all concur to prove her mine; my dear child, whom I left to tafte of misfortune from her cradle!

Molly. [*apart.*] What is he muttering, I wonder! I wifh this one-and-twenty has not turned the old gentleman's head.

Sir

Sir Will. Let me beg the favour of you to conduct me to your miſtreſs : I want to ſpeak with her.

Molly. She will ſee no company, Sir ; ſhe is indiſpoſed ; ſhe is in great affliction ; and receives no viſits at all.

Sir Will. Mine is not a viſit of form or ceremony, or even impertinent curioſity ; but on the moſt urgent buſineſs. Tell her I am her fellow-countryman.

Molly. What ! are you of Scotland too, Sir ?

Sir Will. I am. Tell her I take part in her afflictions, and may, perhaps, bring her ſome conſolation.

Molly. There is ſomething mighty particular about this old gentleman ! He has not brought another two hundred pounds, ſure ! [*Apart.*] Well, Sir ; ſince you are ſo very preſſing, ſince you ſay you are our fellow-countryman, if you will walk this way, I'll ſpeak to my miſtreſs, and ſee what I can do for you.

Sir Will. I am obliged to you. [*Exit Molly.*] And now, if I may truſt the forebodings of an old fond heart, I am going to throw my arms about my daughter. [*Exit.*

As

As Sir William follows Molly out on one side,
Spatter appears on the other.

Spatter alone.

There they go! what the deuce can that old
fellow and Amelia's maid do together? The flut
is certainly conducting him to her miftrefs! In lefs
than half an hour I expect that Amelia will be
apprehended. In the mean time, I muft be upon
the watch; for, fince I have laid the information,
it is high time that I fhould collect fome materials
to fupport it.—Who comes here? Lord Falbridge's
valet de chambre: His errand is to Amelia, without
doubt; fomething may be learnt there, perhaps.

Enter La France.

Ha! Monfieur la France! your fervant.

La. Fr. Serviteur! ver glad to fee you, monfieur Spatter.

Spat. Well; what brings you here? eh, monfieur La France?

La. Fr. Von lettre, monfieur.

Spat. A letter to whom?

La. Fr. From mi lor to Mademoifelle Amelie.

Spat. Oh, you're miftaken, monfieur; that letter
is for lady Alton.

La. Fr. Lady Alton! no, *ma foi!* it be for
Mademoifelle.

Mademoifelle. I am no miftake. *Je ne me trompe
pas la deſſus.*

Spat. Why, have not you carried feveral letters
from lord Falbridge to lady Alton ?

La. Fr. Oh, *que oui !* but dis be for de young
laty dat lif here; for Mademoifelle : Mi lor lov
her ! *ma foi*; he lov her *à la folie.*

Spat. And he loved lady Alton *à la folie,* did
not he ?

La. Fr. Oh, *que non !* he lov her fo *gentely !
ſi tranquilement* ; *ma foi*, he lov her *à la Françoiſe.*
But now he lov Mademoifelle; he no eat, no
fleep, no fpeak, but Mademoifelle ; no tink but of
Mademoifelle ; quite an oder ting, monfieur Spatter, quite an oder ting !

Spat. Well, well; no matter for that; the
letter is for lady Alton, I promife you.

La. Fr. Ah ! *pardonnez moi !*

Spat. It is, I affure you ; and to convince you
of it, fee here, monfieur ! Lady Alton has fent
you five guineas to pay the poftage.

La. Fr. Five guinées ! *ma foi*, I believe I was
miftake, indeed.

Spat. Ay, ay; I told you you were miftaken :
And after all, if it fhould not be for her ladyfhip,
fhe will enclofe it in another cafe, and fend it to
Amelia, and nobody will be the wifer.

La Fr.

La. Fr. Fort *bien*; ver well; *la voilà.* [*gives the letter.*] I have got five guinées; I don't care.

.*Spat.* Why fhould you? Where's the harm, if one woman fhould receive a letter written to another? There will be nothing loft by it; for if Amelia don't receive this, fhe will receive others; and letters of this fort are all alike, you know.

La. Fr. Begar dat is ver true. Adieu, Sir.— I have execute my commiffion: Adieu. *Oh! je fais bien mes commiffions, moi!*   [*Exit.*

Spatter alone.

See the effects of fecret-fervice-money! Intelligence muft be paid for; and the bribing couriers is a fair ftratagem, by all the laws of war. Shall I break open this letter; or carry it to lady Alton as it is? No; I'll read it myfelf, that I may have the credit of communicating the contents. Let me fee! [*opens the letter and reads.*] " Thou dear-" eft, moft refpectable, and moft virtuous of wo-" men!" So! this is *à la folie*, indeed, as monfieur la France calls it.—" If any confideration could " add to my remorfe, for the injury I have offered " you, it would be the difcovery of your real " character." Ah, ah! " I know who you are. " I know you are the daughter of the unhappy " Sir William Douglas." So, fo! "Judge then
                                                        " of

" of the tumult of my foul; which is only pre-
" ferved from the horrors of defpair, by the
" hopes of rendering fome fervice to the father,
" which may, perhaps, in fome meafure atone
" for my behaviour to his too-juftly offended
" daughter. Give me leave, this evening, to fue
" for my pardon at your feet, and to inform you
" of the meafures I have taken. In the mean time,
" believe me unalterably yours. Falbridge."
This is a precious pacquet, indeed.—Now if I
could difcover the father too!—His lordfhip's
vifit will be too late in the evening, I fancy; the
lady will not be at home; but, before fhe goes,
once more to my old trade of eaves-dropping
about her apartments! The old gentleman and fhe
are certainly together, and their converfation perhaps may be curious. At all events, lady Alton
muft be gratified. Men of letters never get any
thing of their patrons, but by facrificing to their
foibles. [*Exit.*

Amelia's apartment.
Sir William Douglas and Amelia difcovered fitting.

Sir Will. Every word you utter, touches me to
the foul. Nothing but fuch noble fentiments
could have fupported your fpirit under fo many
misfortunes.

Amelia. Perhaps it is to my misfortunes that I

E 3 owe

owe thofe fentiments; had I been brought up in eafe and luxury, my mind, which has learnt fortitude from diftrefs, might have been enfeebled by profperity.

Sir Will. Thou moft amiable of thy fex, I conjure thee to hide nothing from me. You fay you were born at Aberdeen; you confefs that you are derived from one of thofe unhappy families, who fuffered themfelves to be fo fatally deluded, and drawn from their allegiance to the beft of kings. Why, why then, will you not tell me all? Why do you endeavour to conceal your name and family?

Amelia. My duty to my family obliges me to filence. My father's life is forfeited by the fentence of the law; and he owes his exiftence at this hour to flight or fecrecy. He may be in England; he may, for aught I know, be in London; and the divulging my name and family might create a frefh fearch after him, and expofe him to new perils. Your converfation, it is true, has infpired me with refpect and tendernefs; but yet you are a ftranger to me: I have reafon to fear every thing, and one word may undo me.

Sir Will. Alas! one word may make us both happy. Tell me; of what age were you, when your cruel fortune feparated you from your father?

Amelia.

Amelia. An infant; fo young, that I have not the leaft traces of him in my memory.

Sir Will. And your mother; what became of her?

Amelia. She, as I have often heard, was carried off by a fever, while fhe was preparing to embark with me, to follow the fortunes of my father. He, driven almoft to defpair by this laft ftroke of ill fortune, continually fhifted his place of refidence abroad; but for fome years paft, whether by his death, the mifcarriage of letters, the infidelity of friends, or other accidents, I have not received the leaft intelligence of him; and now I almoft begin to defpair of hearing of him again, tho' I ftill perfift in my enquiries.

Sir Will. [*rifing.*] It muft be fo; it is as I imagined. All thefe touching circumftances are melancholy witneffes of the truth of it. Yes, my child! I am that unhappy father, whom you loft fo early; I am that unfortunate hufband, whom death and my unhappy fate, almoft at the very fame period, divorced from the beft of wives; I am Sir William Douglas.

Amelia. Sir William Douglas! Have I lived to fee my father? then Heaven has heard my prayers! This is the firft happy moment of my unfortunate

E 4   life.

life. [*embracing*.]—And yet your prefence here fills me with apprehenfions; I tremble for your fafety, for your life; how durft you venture your perfon in this kingdom? how can you expofe yourfelf to the danger of difcovery in this town? My whole foul is in a tumult of fear and joy.

Sir Will. Do not be alarmed, my Amelia; fear nothing; Heaven begins to fmile upon my fortune. To find thee fo unexpectedly, to find thee with a mind fo fuperior to diftrefs, foftens the anguifh of my paft life, and gives me happy omens of the future.

Amelia. Oh, Sir! by the joy I receive from the embraces of a father, let me conjure you to provide for your fafety! do not expofe me to the horror of lofing you again; of lofing you for ever! Quit this town immediately; every moment that you remain in it, is at the hazard of your life; I am ready to accompany you to any part of the world.

Sir Will. My dear child! how I grieve that your youth and virtue fhould be involved in my misfortunes! Yes, we will quit this kingdom; prepare for your departure, and we may leave London this evening.

Enter

Enter Owen haftily.

Ha! Owen! thou art come at a happy moment. I have found my daughter. This is your young miftrefs, the paragon of her fex, my dear, my amiable Amelia!

Owen. Oh, Sir, this is no time for congratulation. You are in the moft imminent danger.

Sir Will. What is the matter?

Owen. The officers of government are at this inftant in the houfe. I faw them enter; I heard them fay they had authority to apprehend fome fufpeᴄᵗed perfon, and I ran immediately to inform you of your danger.

Amelia. Oh, Heaven! My father, what will you do?

Owen. Do not be alarmed, Sir; we are two; we are armed; and we may perhaps be able to make our way through them; I will ftand by you to the laft drop of my blood.

Sir Will. Thou faithful creature! Stay, Owen; our fears may betray us; till we are fure we are attacked, let us fhew no figns of oppofition!

Enter Molly, haftily.

Molly. My dear miftrefs! we are ruined; we are undone for ever.

Amelia.

Amelia. There are officers of juſtice in the houſe; I have heard it : tell me, tell me this inſtant, whom do they ſeek for ?

Molly. For you, madam ; for you ; they have a warrant to apprehend you, they ſay.

Amelia. But they have no warrant to apprehend any body elſe ?

Molly. No, madam ; nobody elſe ; but I will follow you to the end of the world.

Amelia. My dear Polly, I did not mean *you.* Retire, Sir ! [*to Sir William.*] For heaven's leave me to their mercy ; they can have no faƈts againſt me ; my life has been as innocent as unfortunate, and I muſt ſoon be releaſed.

Sir Will. No, my child ; I will not leave thee.

Molly. My child ? This is Sir William Douglas then, as ſure as I am alive !

Sir Will. Beſides, retiring at ſuch a time might create ſuſpicion, and incur the danger we would wiſh to avoid.

Molly. They will be in the room in a moment; I think I hear them upon the ſtairs ; they would have been here before me, if Mr. Freeport had not come in and ſtopt them.

Sir Will. Courage, my dear Amelia !

Amelia. Alas, Sir? I have no terrors but for you.

Owen.

Owen. They are here, Sir.

Molly. Oh, lord! here they are, indeed! I am frighted out of my wits.

Enter Mrs. Goodman, Freeport, and Officer.

Free. A warrant to feize her? a harmlefs young woman? it is impoffible.

Officer. Pardon me, Sir; if the young lady goes by the name of Amelia Walton, I have a warrant to apprehend her.

Free. On what account?

Officer. As a dangerous perfon.

Free. Dangerous!

Officer. Yes, Sir; fufpected of difaffection and treafonable practices.

Amelia. I am the unhappy object of your fearch, Sir; give me leave to know the fubftance of the accufation.

Officer. I cannot tell you particulars, madam; but information upon oath has been made againft you, and I am ordered to apprehend you.

Mrs. Good. But you will accept of bail, Sir? I will be bound for all I am worth in the world.

Officer. In thefe cafes, madam, bail is not ufual; and if ever accepted at all, it is exceffively high;

and

and given by perfons of very large property, and known character.

Free. Well; my property is large enough, and my character very well known. My name is Freeport.

Officer. I know you very well, Sir.

Free. I'll anfwer for her appearance; I'll be bound in a penalty of five hundred pounds, a thoufand, two thoufand, or what fum you pleafe.

Officer. And will you enter into the recognifance immediately?

Free. With all my heart; come along! [*Going.*

Officer. And are you in earneft, Sir?

Free. Ay, to be fure. Why not?

Officer. Becaufe, Sir, I'll venture to fay there are but few people, that place their money on fuch fecurities.

Free. So much the worfe! he who can employ it in doing good, places it on the beft fecurity, and puts it out at the higheft intereft in the world.
[*Exit with the Officer.*

Manent Sir William Douglas, &c.

Sir Will. I can hardly truft my eyes and ears! who is this benevolent gentleman?

Mrs.

Mrs. Good. I don't wonder you are furprifed at Mr. Freeport's manner of proceeding, Sir; but it is his way. He is not a man of compliment; but he does the moft effential fervice, in lefs time than others take in making proteftations.

Molly. Here he is again; heaven reward him!

Re-enter Freeport.

Free. So! that matter is difpatched; now to our other affairs! this is a bufy day with me.—Look-ye, Sir William, we muft be brief; there is no time to be loft.

Sir Will. How! am I betrayed then?

Free. Betrayed! no; but you are difcovered.

Owen. What! my mafter difcovered!

[*Offers to draw.*

Free. [*to Owen.*] Nay, never clap thy hand to thy fword, old Trufty! your mafter is in danger, it is true; but not from me, I promife you. Go, and get him a poft-chaife; and let him pack off this inftant; that is the beft way of fhewing your attachment to him at prefent.—Twenty years, Sir William, have not made fo great an alteration in you, but I knew you the moment I faw you.

Mrs. Good. Harbour no diftruft of Mr. Free-port, Sir; he is one of the worthieft men living.

Amelia.

Amelia. I know his worthinefs. His behaviour to the officer but this moment, uncommonly generous as it appeared, is not the firft teftimony he has given me to-day, of his noble difpofition.

Free. Noble! pfhaw! nonfenfe!

Sir Will. [*to Freeport.*] Sir; the kind manner in which you have been pleafed to intereft yourfelf in my affairs, has almoft as much overpowered me, as if you had furprifed me with hoftile proceedings. Which way fhall I thank you for your goodnefs to me and my Amelia?

Free. Don't thank me at all; when you are out of danger, perhaps I may make a propofal to you, that will not be difagreeable; at prefent, think of nothing but your efcape; for I fhould not be furprifed, if they were very fhortly to make you the fame compliment they have paid to Amelia: and in your cafe, which is really a ferious one, they might not be in the humour to accept of my recognifance.

Mrs. Good. Mr. Freeport is in the right, Sir; every moment of delay is hazardous; let us prevail upon you to depart immediately! Amelia being wholly innocent, cannot be long detained in cuftody, and as foon as fhe is releafed, I will bring her to you, wherever you fhall appoint.

Free.

Free. Ay, ay, you muſt be gone directly, Sir; and as you may want ready money upon the road, take my purſe!   [*Offering his purſe.*

Sir Will. No, thou trueſt friend, I have no need of it. With what wonderful goodneſs have you acted towards me and my unhappy family!

Free. Wonderful! why wonderful? Would not you have done the ſame, if you had been in my place?

Sir Will. I hope I ſhould.

Free. Well then, where is the wonder of it? Come, come, let us ſee you make ready for your departure!

Sir Will. Thou beſt of men!

Free. Beſt of men? Heaven forbid! I have done no more than my duty by you. I am a man myſelf; and am bound to be a friend to all mankind, you know.   [*Exeunt.*

A C T

A C T IV.

SCENE, *Spatter's apartment.*
Lady Alton with a letter in her hand, and Spatter.
Lady Alton.

THANKS, my good Spatter, many thanks for this precious epiſtle! more precious at preſent than one of Ovid, Pliny, or Cicero. It is at once a billet-doux and a ſtate paper; and ſerves at the ſame time to convict her of conſpiring againſt me and the publick.

Spat. It is a valuable manuſcript, to be ſure, madam; and yet that is but the leaſt half of my diſcoveries, ſince I left your ladyſhip.

L. Alt. But is not this half, according to the Grecian axiom, more than the whole, Mr. Spatter?

Spat. When you know the whole, I believe you will think not, madam.

L. Alt. Out with it then! I am impatient to be miſtreſs of it.

Spat. By intercepting this letter of lord Falbridge's, your ladyſhip ſees that we have diſcovered Amelia to be the daughter of Sir William Douglas.

L. Alt.

L. Alt. True.

Spat. But what would you fay, madam, if I had found out the father himfelf too?

L. Alt. Sir William Douglas!

Spat. Is now in this houfe, madam.

L. Alt. Impoffible!

Spat. Nothing more certain. He arrived this morning, under a feigned name. I faw him conducted to Amelia's apartment. This raifed my fufpicion, and I planted myfelf at her door, with all the circumfpection of a fpy, and addrefs of a chambermaid. There I overheard their mutual acknowledgments of each other; and a curious interview it was. Firft they wept for grief; and then they wept for joy; and then they wept for grief again. Their tears, however, were foon interrupted by the arrival of the officer, whofe purpofe was partly defeated, as you have already heard, by the intervention of Freeport.

L. Alt. Yes; the brute! But that delay was not half fo unfortunate, as your difcoveries have been happy, Spatter; for my revenge fhall now return on them with redoubled fury. Iffue out upon them once more; fee what they are about; and be fure to give me immediate notice if lord Falbridge fhould come.   [*Going.*

Spat. Stay, madam. After intercepting the letter, I fent for your ladyſhip, that at ſo critical a juncture, you might be preſent on the ſpot: and if you go home again, we ſhall loſe time, which perhaps may be precious, in running to and fro. Suppoſe you ſtep into the ſtudy, till I return. You will find my own anſwer to my laſt pamphlet, and the two firſt ſheets of the next month's magazine, to amuſe you.

L. Alt. Planned like a wiſe general! Do you then go, and *reconnoitre* the enemy, while I lie here in ambuſh to reinforce you as ſoon as there ſhall be occaſion. Do but give the word, we'll make a vigorous ſally, put their whole body to rout, and take Amelia and her father priſoners.

[*Exeunt ſeverally.*

A hall.

Freeport alone.

I don't know how it is; but this Amelia here runs in my head ſtrangely. Ever ſince I ſaw her, I think of nothing elſe. I am not in love with her. In love with her! that's nonſenſe. But I feel a kind of uneaſineſs, a ſort of pain that—I don't know what to make of it—I'll ſpeak to her father about her.

Enter

Enter Owen.

Well, old True-penny! Have you prepared every thing for Sir William's departure?

Owen. We had need be going, indeed, Sir; we are in continual danger while we ftay here. Who d'ye think lodged the information againft madam Amelia?

Free. Who?

Owen. A perfon who lodges in this very houfe, it feems: One Mr. Spatter, Sir.

Free. Spatter! how d'ye know?

Owen. I had it from one of the officers who came to apprehend her.

Free. A dog! I could find in my heart to cut off his ears with my own hands, and fave him the difgrace of the pillory.

Owen. My poor mafter is always unfortunate. If lord Brumpton had lived a week longer, Sir William might perhaps have been out of the reach of their malice.

Free. Lord Brumpton?

Owen. Yes, Sir. He was foliciting my mafter's pardon; but died before he had accomplifhed his benevolent intentions.

Free. Ha! a thought ftrikes me. [*Apart.*] Hark

ye,

ye, friend, [*to Owen*] does Sir William know the prefent Lord Brumpton ?

Owen. No, Sir. The late lord had no children, or near relations, living ; and, indeed, he was the only furviving friend of my poor mafter in the kingdom.

Free. Is the chaife at the door ?

Owen. Not yet, Sir ; but I expect it every moment.

Free. Run to your mafter, and defire him not to go till I fee him. Tell him I am going out upon his bufinefs, and will be back within this hour.

Owen. I will let him know immediately. Ah, you're a true friend indeed, Sir.

> [*Shaking him earneftly by the hand.*

Free. Pho, prithee !

Owen. Ah ! Heaven preferve you !   [*Exit.*

Freeport alone.

Fare thee well, old Honefty ! By the death of lord Brumpton, without children or near relations living, as Owen fays, the title and eftate come to my old friend Jack Brumpton, of Liverpoole ; who is of a diftant branch ; a fortieth coufin, for aught I know ; who has paft his whole life in a counting-houfe ; and who, a few years ago, no

more

more dreamt of being a lord, than grand fignior, or great mogul. He has fo good a heart, that I believe it is impoffible even for a title to corrupt it. I know he is in town; fo I'll go to him immediately; acquaint him with the obligation entailed on him, to be of fervice to Sir William; and make him heir to the benevolence of his predeceffor, as well as his wealth and dignity. [*Going, ftops.*] Who's here! Mrs. Goodman and Spatter, as I live! Oh, the dog! my blood rifes at the villain. If I don't take care, I fhall incur an action of battery for caning the rafcal.

Enter Mrs. Goodman and Spatter.

Mrs. Good. In fhort, Mr. Spatter, I muft beg leave to give you warning, and defire that you would provide yourfelf with another lodging as foon as poffible.

Spat. What now? what the deuce is the matter with you, Mrs. Goodman?

Mrs. Good. I fee now the meaning of lady Alton's recommendation of fuch a lodger to my houfe, as well as of her vifits to Amelia, and her frequent conferences with you, Sir.

Spat. The woman is certainly out of her fenfes.

Free. -

Free. What has been laid to your charge is no joke, Sir.

Spat. What! are you there to keep up her back-hand, Mr. Freeport? What is all this?

Free. You are found out to be a fpy, Sir.

Mrs. Good. A perfon who pries into the fecrets of families, merely to betray them.

Free. An informer.

Mrs. Good. An eaves-dropper.

Free. A liar.

Spat. Right-hand and left! this is too much: what the plague is the matter with you both!

Mrs. Good. Did not you go and tell that Amelia was a native of Scotland?

Spat. Well; and where's the harm of being born in Scotland?

Free. None; except by your malicious interpre-tation, rafcal; by means of which you made it the ground of an information againft her, and were the caufe of her being apprehended.

Spat. And you were the caufe of her being re-leafed; every man in his way, Mr. Freeport!

Free. Look you, firrah! you are one of thofe wretches, who mifcall themfelves authors; a fel-low, whofe heart, and tongue, and pen, are equally fcandalous; who try to infinuate yourfelf every

where,

where, to make mifchief if there is none, and to increafe it, if you find any. But if you fetch and carry like a fpaniel, you muft be treated like one. I have obferved that you are always loitering in the paffages; but if I catch you within the wind of a door again, I'll beat you till you are as black as your own ink, firrah, Now you know my mind.

[*Exit.*

Spat. Very civil and very polite, indeed, Mr. Freeport. Ha! here comes my friend lord Falbridge.

Mrs. Good. Lord Falbridge your friend? For fhame, Mr. Spatter!

Enter Lord Falbridge, haftily.

L. Fal. Mrs. Goodman, I rejoice to fee you. Tell me, how does my Amelia? I have heard of her diftrefs, and flew to her relief. Was fhe alarmed? was fhe terrified?

Mrs. Good. Not much, my lord: She fuftained the fhock with the fame conftancy that fhe endures every other affliction.

L. Fal. I know her merit; I am too well acquainted with her greatnefs of foul; and hope it is not yet too late for me to do juftice to her virtue. Go to her, my dear Mrs. Goodman, and tell her, I beg to fee her: I have fomething that concerns her very nearly, to impart to her.

Mrs,

Mrs. Good. I will, my lord.   [*Exit.*

L. Fal. Oh, Mr. Spatter! I did not fee you. What have you got there, Sir?

[*Seeing a paper in his hand.*

Spat. Propofals for a new work, my lord! May I beg the honour of your lordfhip's name among my lift of fubfcribers?

L. Fal. With all my heart, Sir. I am already in your debt on another account.

[*Pulling out his purfe.*

Spat. To me, my lord? You do me a great deal of honour; I fhould be very proud to be of the leaft fervice to your lordfhip.

L. Fal. You have been of great fervice to me already, Sir. It was you, I find, lodged the information againft this young lady.

Spat. I did no more than my duty, my lord.

L. Fal. Yes; you did me a favour, Sir. I confider only the deed, and put the intention quite out of the queftion. You meant to do Amelia a prejudice, and you have done me a fervice: for by endeavouring to bring her into diftrefs, you gave me an opportunity of fhewing my eagernefs to relieve her.—There, Sir! there is for the good you have done, while you meant to make mifchief. [*giving him a few guineas.*] But take this along with it; if you ever prefume to mention the name

of

of Amelia any more, or give yourſelf the leaſt
concern about her, or her affairs, I'll——

Spat. I am obliged to your lordſhip. [*Bowing.*

L. Fal. Be gone, Sir; leave me.

Spat. Your moſt humble ſervant, my lord!——
So; I am abuſed by every body; and yet I get
money by every body;—egad, I believe I am a
much cleverer fellow than I thought I was. [*Exit.*

Lord Falbridge alone.

Alas! I am afraid that Amelia will not ſee me.
What would I not ſuffer to repair the affront that
I have offered her?

Enter Molly.

Ha! Polly! how much am I obliged to you
for ſending me notice of Amelia's diſtreſs!

Molly. Huſh, my lord! Speak lower, for heaven's fake! My miſtreſs has ſo often forbad me
to tell any thing about her, that I tremble ſtill at
the thoughts of the confidence I have put in you.
I was bewitched, I think, to let you know who
ſhe was.

L. Fal. You were inſpired, Polly; heaven inſpired you to acquaint me with all her diſtreſſes,
that I might recommend myſelf to her favour
again,

again, by my zeal to ferve her, though againſt her will.

Molly. That was the reaſon I told you; for elſe I am ſure I ſhould die with grief to give her the leaſt uneaſineſs.

L. Fal. But may I hope to ſee Amelia? Will ſhe let me ſpeak with her?

Molly. No indeed, my lord; ſhe is ſo offended at your late behaviour, that ſhe will not even ſuffer us to mention your name to her.

L. Fal. Death and confuſion! What a wretch have I made myſelf! Go, Polly, go, and let her know that I muſt ſpeak with her; inform her, that I have been active for her welfare; and have authority to releaſe her from the information lodged againſt her.

Molly. I will let her know your anxiety, my lord; but indeed I am afraid ſhe will not ſee you.

L. Fal. She muſt, Polly, ſhe muſt. The agonies of my mind are intolerable; tell her, ſhe muſt come, if it be but for a moment; or elſe, in the bitter-neſs of deſpair, I fear I ſhall break into her apart-ment, and throw myſelf at her feet.

Molly. Lud! you frighten me out of my wits. Have a little patience, and I'll tell my miſtreſs what a taking you are in.

L. Fal.

L. Fal. Fly, then! I can tafte no comfort, till I hear her refolution. [*Exit Molly.*

Lord Falbridge alone.

How culpably have I acted towards the moft amiable of her fex! But I will make her every reparation in my power. The warmth and fince-rity of my repentance fhall extort forgivenefs from her. By heaven, fhe comes!—Death! how fenfi-bly does an ungenerous action abafe us! I am confcious of the fuperiority of her virtue, and almoft dread the encounter.

Enter Amelia.

Amelia. I underftand, my lord, that by your application I am held free of the charge laid againft me; and that I am once more entirely at liberty. I am truly fenfible of your good offices, and thank you for the trouble you have taken. [*Going.*

L. Fal. Stay, madam! do not leave me in ftill greater diftraction than you found me. If my zeal to ferve you has had any weight with you, it muft have infpired you with more favourable difpo-fitions towards me.

Amelia. You muft pardon me, my lord, if I çannot fo foon forget a very late tranfaction. After

that,

that, all your proceedings alarm me : Nay, even your prefent zeal to ferve me creates new ſuſpicions, while I cannot but be doubtful of the motives from which it proceeds.

L. Fal. Cruel Amelia ! for, guilty as I am, I muſt complain, ſince it was your own diffidence that was in part the occaſion of my crime.—Why did you conceal your rank and condition from me ? Why did not you tell me, that you were the daughter of the unhappy Sir William Douglas ?

Amelia. Who told you that I was ſo, my lord ?

L. Fal. Nay, do not deny it now : it is in vain to attempt to conceal it any longer ; it was the main purport of my letter to apprize you of my knowledge of it.

Amelia. Your letter, my lord !

L. Fal. Yes ; wild as it was, it was the offſpring of compunction and remorſe ; and if it conveyed the dictates of my ſoul, it ſpoke me the trueſt of penitents. You did not diſdain to read it, ſure !

Amelia. Indeed, my lord, I never received any letter from you.

L. Fal. Not received any ! I ſent it this very morning. My own ſervant was the meſſenger. What can this mean ? Has he betrayed me ?—At

preſent,

prefent, fuffer me to compenfate, as far as poffible, for the wrongs I have done you : Receive my hand and heart, and let an honourable marriage obliterate the very idea of my paft conduct.

Amelia. No, my lord ; you have difcovered me, it is true : I am the daughter of Sir William Douglas. Judge for yourfelf then ; and think how I ought to look upon a man, who has infulted my diftrefs, and endeavoured to tempt me to difhonour my family.

L. Fal. Your juftice muft acquit me of the intention of that offence, fince at that time I was ignorant of your illuftrious extraction.

Amelia. It may be fo ; yet your excufe is but an aggravation of the crime. You imagined me, perhaps, to be of as low and mean an origin, as you thought me poor and unhappy. You fuppofed that I had no title to any dowry but my honour, no dependance but on my virtue; and yet you attempted to rob me of that virtue, which was the only jewel that could raife the meannefs of my birth, or fupport me under my misfortunes ; which, inftead of relieving, you chofe to make the pandar to your vile inclinations.

L. Fal. Thou moft amiable of thy fex, how I adore thee ! Even thy refentment renders thee

more

more lovely in my eyes, and makes thee, if poffible, dearer to me than ever. Nothing but our
union can ever make me happy.

Amelia. Such an union muſt not, cannot be.

L. Fal. Why ? what ſhould forbid it ?

Amelia. My father.

L. Fal. Your father ! where is he ? In whatever
part of the world he now reſides, I will convey you
to him, and he ſhall ratify our happineſs.

Enter Molly, haſtily.

Molly. Oh lord, madam ! here's the angry lady
coming again ; ſhe that made ſuch a racket this
morning.

Amelia. Lady Alton ?

Molly. Yes, madam.

L. Fal. Lady Alton ! Confuſion ! Stay, madam.
[*To Amelia, who is going.*

Amelia. No, my lord ; I have endured one affront from her already to-day ; why ſhould I ex-
poſe myſelf to a ſecond ? Her ladyſhip, you know,
has a prior claim to your attention. [*Exit.*

L. Fal. Diſtraction ! I had a thouſand things to
ſay to her.—Go, my dear Polly, follow my Amelia !
Plead earneſtly in my behalf ; urge all the ten-
dereſt things that fancy can ſuggeſt, and return to
me as ſoon as lady Alton is departed !

Molly.

Molly. I will, my lord. O lud! here she is, as I am alive! [*Exit.*

L. Fal. Abandoned by Amelia! and hunted by this fury! I shall run wild.

Enter lady Alton.

L. Alt. You may well turn away from me; at length, I have full conviction of your basenefs. I am now affured of my own shame, and your falsehood. Perfidious monster!

L. Fal. It is unjust to tax me with perfidy, madam. I have rather acted with too much fincerity. I long ago frankly declared to you the utter impoffibility of our reconciliation.

L. Alt. What! after having made your addreffes to me? After having fworn the moft inviolable affection for me? Oh, thou arch deceiver!

L. Fal. I never deceived you: when I profeffed a paffion, I really entertained one; when I made my addreffes to you, I wished to call you my wife.

L. Alt. And what can you allege in excuse of your falfhood? Have you not been guilty of the blackeft perjury?

L. Fal. The change of my fentiments needs no excuse from me, madam; you were yourfelf the

occafion

occafion of it.—In fpite of the torrent of fafhion, and the practice of too many others of my rank in life, I have a relifh for domeftick happinefs; and have always wifhed for a wife, who might render my home a delightful refuge from the cares and buftle of the world abroad. Thefe were my views with you; but, thank heaven, your outrageous temper happily betrayed itfelf in good time, and convinced me that my fole aim in marriage would be fruftrated: for I could neither have been happy myfelf, nor have made you fo.

L. Alt. Paltry evafion! You have abandoned me for your Amelia; you have meanly quitted a perfon of letters, a woman of rank and condition, for an illiterate vagabond, a needy adventurer.

L. Fal. The perfon you mention, madam, is, indeed, the oppofite of yourfelf; fhe is all meeknefs, grace, and virtue.

L. Alt. Provoking traitor! You urge me paft all fufferance. I meant to expoftulate, but you oblige me to invective.—But, have a care! You are not fo fecure as you fuppofe yourfelf; and I may revenge myfelf fooner than you imagine.

L. Fal. I am aware of your vindictive difpofition, madam; for I know that you are more envious than jealous, and rather violent than tender; but

the

the prefent object of my affections fhall be placed above your refentment, and challenge your refpect.

L. Alt. Away, fond man! I know that object of your affections better than yourfelf; I know who fhe is; I know who the ftranger is that arrived for her this morning; I know all: men more powerful than yourfelf fhall be apprifed of the whole immediately; and within thefe two hours, nay, within this hour, you fhall fee the unworthy object, for which you have flighted me, with all that is dear to her and you, torn away from you perforce.   [*going.*

L. Fal. Ha! how's this? Stay, madam! Explain yourfelf! But one word; do but hear me!

L. Alt. No; I difdain to hear you: I fcorn all explanation. I have difcovered the contemptible caufe of your inconftancy, and know you to be mean, bafe, falfe, treacherous, and perfidious. You have forfeited my tendernefs, and be affured you fhall feel the effects of my revenge.   [*Exit.*

L. Fal. What does fhe mean? The ftranger that arrived to-day!—That arrived for my Amelia!—Sure it cannot be. [*Paufing.*] Is it poffible that————[*Re-enter Molly.*] Ha, Polly! explain thefe riddles to me. Lady Alton threatens me; fhe threatens my Amelia: does fhe know any

VOL. II.   G   thing?

thing ? Her fury will tranfport her to every extravagance ! How dreadful is jealoufy in a woman !.

Molly. Ay, it is a dreadful thing, indeed, my lord. Well! heaven fend me always to be in love, and never to be jealous !

L. Fal. But fhe talked of tearing Amelia from me perforce—And then, fome ftranger—She threatens *him* too : what is it fhe means ?

Molly. What ! a gentleman that came to madam Amelia ?   [*alarmed.*

L. Fal. Yes, to Amelia ; and arrived this very day, fhe fays.

Molly. We are ruined for ever : fhe means Sir William Douglas !

L. Fal. The father of my Amelia ! Is he here ?

Molly. Yes, my lord ; I was bound to fecrecy : but I can't help telling you the whole truth, becaufe I am fure you will do all in your power to be of fervice to us.

L. Fal. You know my whole foul, Polly : this outrageous woman's malice fhall be defeated.

Molly. Heaven fend it may !

L. Fal. Be affured, it fhall : do not alarm your miftrefs ; I fly to ferve her, and will return as foon as poffible.

Molly. I fhall be miferable till we fee you again, my lord.

L. Fal.

L. Fal. And now, good heaven! that art the protection of innocence, fecond my endeavours! enable me to repair the affront I have offered to injured virtue, and let me relieve the unhappy from their diftreffes! [*Exeunt feverally.*

A C T V.

SCENE *continues.*

Lord Falbridge and Molly meeting.

Molly. OH, my lord! I am glad to fee you returned.

L. Fal. Where is your miftrefs? [*eagerly.*

Molly. In her own chamber.

L. Fal. And where is Sir William Douglas?

Molly. With my miftrefs.

L. Fal. And have there been no officers here to apprehend them?

Molly. Officers! No, my lord. Officers! You frighten me. I was in hopes, by feeing your lordfhip fo foon again, that there were fome good news for us.

L. Fal. Never was any thing fo unfortunate.

The

The noble perfons, to whom I meant to make ap‑
plication, were out of town ; nor could by any
means be feen or fpoken with, till to‑morrow.
morning : And to add to my diftraction, I learnt
that a new information had been made, and a new
warrant iffued, to apprehend Sir William Douglas
and Amelia.

Molly. Oh dear ! what can we do then ?

L. Fal. Do ! I fhall run mad. Go, my dear
Polly, go to your miftrefs and Sir William, and
inform them of their danger. Every moment
is precious ; but perhaps they may yet have time
to efcape.

Molly. I will, my lord ! [*going.*

L. Fal. Stay ! [*Molly returns.*] My chariot is at
the door ; tell them, not to wait for any other
carriage, but to get into that, and drive away im‑
mediately.

Molly. I will, my lord. Oh dear ! I never was
fo terrified in all my life. [*Exit.*

Lord Falbridge alone.

If I can but fave them now, we may gain time
for mediation. Ha ! what noife ? Are the officers
coming ? Who's here ?

Enter

Enter La France.

La Fr. Mi lor, Monf. le duc de——

L. Fal. Sirrah! villain! you have been the occafion of all this mifchief. By your careleffnefs, or treachery, lady Alton has intercepted my letter to Amelia.

La Fr. Lèdy Altón?

L. Fal. Yes, dog; did not I fend you here this morning with a letter?

La Fr. Oui, mi lor.

L. Fal. And did you bring it here, rafcal?

La Fr. Oui, mi lor.

L. Fal. No, firrah. You did not bring it; the lady never received any letter from me; fhe told me fo herfelf. Whom did you give it to? [*La France hefitates.*] Speak, firrah; or I'll fhake your foul out of your body.   [*Shaking him.*

La Fr. I giv it to——

L. Fal. Who, rafcal?

La Fr. Monfieur Spatter.

L. Fal. Mr. Spatter?

La Fr. Oui, mi lor; he promis to giv it to Mademoifelle Amelie, vid his own hand.

L. Fal. I fhall foon know the truth of that, Sir, for yonder is Mr. Spatter himfelf: run, and tell him I defire to fpeak with him!

La Fr.

La Fr. Oui, mi lor. *Ma foi,* I vas very near kefh;
I never was in more *vilain embarras* in all my life.
[*Exit.*

Lord Falbridge alone.

My letter's falling into the hands of that fellow
accounts for every thing. The contents inftructed
him concerning Amelia. What a wretch I am!
Deftined every way to be of prejudice to that virtue, which I am bound to adore.

Re-enter La France with Spatter.

Spat. Monfieur La France tells me that your
lordfhip defires to fpeak with me; what are your
commands, my lord? [*Pertly.*

L. Fal. The eafy impudence of the rafcal puts
me out of all patience. [*To himfelf.*

Spat. My lord!

L. Fal. The laft time I faw you, Sir, you were
rewarded for the good you had done; you muft
expect now to be chaftifed for your mifchief.

Spat. Mifchief, my lord?

L. Fal. Yes, Sir; where is that letter of mine,
which La France tells me he gave you to deliver
to a young lady of this houfe?

Spat. Oh, the devil! [*apart.*] Letter, my lord?
[*Hefitates.*
L. Fal.

L. Fal. Yes, letter, Sir; did not you give it him, La France?

La Fr. Oui, mi lor!

Spat. Y—e—e—s, yes, my lord; I had the letter of monfieur La France, to be fure, my lord; but——but——

L. Fal. But what, firrah? Give me the letter immediately; and if I find that the feal has been broken, I will break every bone in your fkin.

Spat. For Heaven's fake, my lord! [*feeling in his pockets.*] I—I—I— have not got the letter about me at prefent, my lord; but if you will give me leave to ftep to my apartment, I'll bring it you immediately. [*Offering to go.*

L. Fal. [*Stopping him.*] No, no; that will not do, Sir; you fhall not ftir, I promife you. Look you, rafcal! tell me what is become of my letter, or I will be the death of you this inftant. [*Drawing.*

Spat. [*kneeling.*] Put up your fword, my lord; put up your fword; and I will tell you every thing in the world; indeed, I will.

L. Fal. Well, Sir; be quick then!

[*Putting up his fword.*

Spat. Lady Alton——

L. Fal. Lady Alton! I thought fo; go on, Sir.

Spat. Lady Alton, my lord, defired me to pro-

cure

cure her all the intelligence in my power, concerning every thing that paſt between your lordſhip
and Amelia.

L. Fal. Well, Sir; what then?

Spat. A little patience, I entreat your lordſhip.
Accordingly, to oblige her ladyſhip—one muſt
oblige the ladies, you know, my lord—I did keep
a pretty ſharp look-out, I muſt confeſs: And this
morning, meeting monſieur La France, with a letter from your lordſhip in his charge, I very readily
gave him five guineas of her ladyſhip's bounty-
money, to put it into my hands.

La Fr. Ob diable! me voila perdu!   [*Aſide.*

L. Fal. How! a bribe, raſcal?   [*To La France.*

La Fr. Ah, mi lor!   [*On his knees.*

Spat. At the ſame price for every letter, he
would have ſold a whole mail, my lord.

   La Fr. Ayez pitié de moi! [*Holding up his hands.*

L. Fal. Betray the confidence I repoſed in you?

Spat. He offered me the letter of his own ac-
cord, my lord.

La Fr. No ſuch ting, en verité, mi lor!

Spat. Very true, I can aſſure your lordſhip.

L. Fal. Well, well; I ſhall chaſtiſe him at my
leiſure. At preſent, Sir, do you return me my
letter.

                                        Spat.

Spat. I—I have it not about me, my lord.

L. Fal. Where is it, rafcal? tell me this inftant, or——

La Fr. Lèdy Altón——

L. Fal. [*To Spatter.*] What! has *fhe* got it? fpeak, firrah!

Spat. She has, indeed, my lord.

L. Fal. Are not you a couple of villains?

La Fr. Oui, mi lor. ⎫
Spat. Yes, my lord! ⎬ *Both fpeak at once.*
⎭

L. Fal. [*To Spatter.*] But hold, Sir! a word more with you! As you feem to be lady Alton's chief agent, I muft defire fome further information from you.

Spat. Any thing in my power, my lord.

L. Fal. I can account for her knowledge of Amelia, by means of my letter: But how did fhe difcover Sir William Douglas?

Spat. I told her, my lord.

L. Fal. But how did you difcover him yourfelf?

Spat. By liftening, my lord.

L. Fal. By liftening?

Spat. Yes, by liftening, my lord! Let me but once be about a houfe, and I'll engage to clear it, like a ventilator, my lord. There is not a door to a fingle apartment in this houfe, but I have planted my ear at the keyhole.

L. Fal.

L. Fal. And were thefe the means by which you procured your intelligence?

Spat. Yes, my lord.

L. Fal. Impoffible.

Spat. Oh dear! nothing fo eafy; this is nothing at all, my lord! I have given an account of the plays in our journal, for three months together, without being nearer the ftage than the pit-paffage; and I have collected the debates of a whole feffion, for the magazine, only by attending in the lobby.

L. Fal. Precious rafcal! Ha! who comes here? lady Alton herfelf again, as I live!

Spat. [*Apart.*] The devil fhe is! I wifh I was out of the houfe.

Enter Lady Alton.

L. Alt. What! ftill here, my lord? ftill witneffing to your own fhame, and the juftice of my refent-ment?

L. Fal. Yes, I am ftill here, madam; and forry to be made a witnefs of your cruelty and mean-nefs; of your defcending to arts, fo much beneath your rank; and practices, fo unworthy of your fex.

L. Alt. You talk in riddles, my lord!

L. Fal. This gentleman fhall explain them. Here, madam! here is the engine of your malice,

the

the inftrument of your vengeance, your prime minifter, Mr. Spatter.

L. Alt. What have I to do with Mr. Spatter?

L. Fal. To do mifchief; to intercept letters, and break them open; to overhear private conver-fations, and betray them; to——

L. Alt. Have you laid any thing of this kind to my charge, Sir?   [*To Spatter.*

Spat. I have been obliged to fpeak the truth, though much againft my will, indeed, madam.

L. Alt. The truth! thou father of lies, did ever any truth proceed from thee? What! is his lord-fhip your new patron! A fit Mæcenas for thee, thou fcandal to the *belles lettres!*

L. Fal. Your rage at this detection is but a frefh conviction of your guilt.

L. Alt. Do not triumph, monfter! you fhall ftill feel the fuperiority I have over you. The ob-ject of your wifhes is no longer under your protec-tion; the officers of the government entered the houfe at the fame time with myfelf, with a war-rant to feize both Amelia and her father.

L. Fal. Confufion! Are not they gone then? La France! villain, run, and bring me word!

La Fr. I go, mi lor!   [*Exit.*

L. Alt. Do not flatter yourfelf with any hopes;
                           they

they have not efcaped; here they are, fecured in proper hands.

L. Fal. Death and diftraction! now I am completely miferable.

Enter Sir William Douglas, Amelia, Owen, and Officers.

L. Alt. Yes, your mifery is complete indeed; and fo fhall be my revenge. Oh! your fervant, madam! [*turning to Amelia*] You now fee to what a condition your pride and obftinacy have reduced you. Did not I bid you tremble at the confequences?

Amelia. It was here alone that I was vulnerable. [*holding her father's hand.*] Oh, madam, [*turning to lady Alton*] by the virtues that fhould adorn your rank, by the tendernefs of your fex, I conjure you, pity my diftrefs! do but releafe my father; and there are no conceffions, however humiliating, which you may not exact from me.

L. Alt. Thofe conceffions now come too late, madam. If I were even inclined to relieve you, at prefent, it is not in my power. [*haughtily.*] Lord Falbridge perhaps may have more intereft.

[*With a fneer.*

L. Fal. Cruel, infulting woman! [*to lady Alton.*]
Do

Do not alarm yourfelf, my Amelia! Do not be concerned, Sir! [*to Sir William.*] Your enemies fhall ftill be difappointed. Altho' ignorant of your arrival, I have for fome time paft exerted all my intereft in your favour, and by the mediation of thofe ftill more powerful, I do not defpair of fuccefs. Your cafe is truly a compaffionate one; and in that breaft, from which alone mercy can proceed, thank heaven, there is the greateft reafon to expect it.

Sir Will. I am obliged to you for your concern, Sir.

L. Fal. Oh, I owe you all this, and much more. —But this is no time to fpeak of my offences, or repentance.

L. Alt. 'This is mere trifling. I thought you knew on what occafion you came hither, Sir.

[*To the Officer.*

Officer. Your reproof is too juft, madam. I attend you, Sir.   [*To Sir William.*

L. Fal. Hold! Let me prevail on you, Sir, [*to the officer*] to fuffer them to remain here till to-morrow morning. I will anfwer for the confequences.

Officer. Pardon me, my lord! we fhould be happy to oblige you; but we muft difcharge the duty of our office.

L. Fal.

L. Fal. Diftraction!

Sir Will. Come then! we follow you, Sir! Be comforted, my Amelia! for my fake, be comforted! Wretched as I am, your anxiety fhocks me more than my own misfortunes.

[*As they are going out, enter* Freeport.

Free. Heyday! what now! the officers here again! I thought we had fatisfied you this morning. What is the meaning of all this?

Officer. This will inform you, Sir.

[*giving the warrant.*

Free. How's this? Let me fee! [*reading.*] *This is to require you*—um, um—*the bodies of William Ford and Amelia Walton*—um, um—*fufpeƈted perfons*—um, um—Well, well! I fee what this is: but you will accept of bail, Sir!

Officer. No, Sir; this cafe is not bailable, and we have already been reprimanded for taking your recognifance this morning.

Sir Will. Thou good man! I fhall ever retain the moft lively fenfe of your behaviour; but your kind endeavours to preferve the poor remainder of my profcribed life are in vain. We muft fubmit to our deftiny.   [*All going.*

Free. Hold, hold! one word, I befeech you, Sir! [*to the officer*] a minute or two will make no difference. Bail then, it feems, will not do, Sir?

Officer.

Officer. No, Sir.

Free. Well, well; then I have fomething here that will, perhaps. [*Feeling in his pocket.*

L. Fal. How !

L. Alt. What does he mean ?

Free. No, it is not there—It is in t'other pocket, I believe. Here, Sir William ! [*producing a parchment.*] Afk the gentlemen, if *that* will not do. —But firft of all, read it yourfelf, and let us hear how you like the contents.

Sir Will. What do I fee ! [*opening and perufing it.*] My pardon ! the full and free pardon of my of- fences ! Oh, heaven ! and is it to you then, to you, Sir, that I owe all this ?—Thus, thus let me fhew my gratitude to my benefactor !

[*Falling at his feet.*

Free. Get up, get up, Sir William ! Thank hea- ven, and the moft gracious of monarchs. You have very little obligation to me, I promife you.

Amelia. My father reftored ! Then I am the hap- pieft of women.

L. Fal. A pardon ! I am tranfported.

L. Alt. How's this ? a pardon !

Free. Under the great feal, madam.

L. Alt. Confufion ! what ! am I baffled at laft, then ? Am I difappointed even of my revenge ?—

'Thou

Thou officious fool! [*to Freeport.*] May thefe wretches prove as great a torment to you, as they have been to me! As for thee, [*to lord Falbridge.*] thou perfidious monfter, may thy guilt prove thy punifhment! May you obtain the unworthy union you defire! May your wife prove as falfe to you, as you have been to me! May you be followed, like Oreftes, with the furies of a guilty confcience; find your error when it is too late; and die in all the horrors of defpair!   [*Exit.*

Free. There goes a woman of quality for you! What little actions, and what a great foul!—Ha! Mafter Spatter! where are you going?

                    [*To Spatter, who is fneaking off.*

Spat. Following the mufe, Sir! [*pointing after lady Alton.*] But if you have any further commands, or his lordfhip fhould have occafion for me to write his epithalamium————

L. Fal. Peace, wretch! fleep in a whole fkin, and be thankful! I would folicit mercy myfelf, and have not leifure to punifh you. Begone, Sir!

Spat. I am obliged to your lordfhip.—This affair will make a good article for the Evening-Poft to-night, however.   [*Afide, and exit.*

Sir Will. How happy has this reverfe of fortune made me!—But my furprize is almoft equal to my

                                   joy.

joy. May we beg you, Sir, [*to Freeport.*] to inform us how your benevolence has effected what seems almost a miracle in my favour?

Free. In two words then, Sir William, this happy event is chiefly owing to your old friend, the late lord Brumpton.

Sir Will. Lord Brumpton!

Free. Yes; honest Owen there told me, that his lordship had been employed in soliciting your pardon. Did not you, Owen?

Owen. I did, Sir.

Free. Upon hearing that, and perceiving the danger you were in, I went immediately to the present lord Brumpton, who is a very honest fellow, and one of the oldest acquaintance I have in the world. He, at my instance, immediately made the necessary application; and guess how agreeably we were surprised, to hear that the late lord had already been successful, and that the pardon had been made out, on the very morning of the day his lordship died. Away went I, as fast as a pair of horses could carry me, to fetch it; and should certainly have prevented this last arrest, if the warrant to apprehend you, as dangerous persons, had not issued under your assumed names of William Ford and Amelia Walton, against whom the information had been laid. But, however, it has only ſerved to prevent your running away, when the danger was over, for at preſent, Sir William, thank heaven and his majeſty, you are a whole man again; and you have nothing to do but to make a legal appearance, and to plead the pardon I have brought you, to abſolve you from all informations.

L. Fal. Thou honeſt excellent man! How happily have you ſupplied, what I failed to accompliſh!

Free. Ay, I heard that your lordſhip had been buſy.—You had more friends at court than one, Sir William, I promiſe you.

Sir Will. I am overwhelmed with my ſudden good fortune, and am poor even in thanks. Teach me, Mr. Freeport, teach me how to make ſome acknowledgment for your extraordinary generoſity!

Free. I'll tell you what, Sir William. Notwithſtanding your daughter's pride, I took a liking to her, the moment I ſaw her.

L. Fal. Ha! what's this?

Free. What's the matter, my lord?

- *L. Fal.* Nothing. Go on, Sir!

Free. Why then, to confeſs the truth, I am afraid that my benevolence, which you have all been pleaſed to praiſe ſo highly, had ſome little leaven of ſelf-intereſt in it; and I was deſirous

to

to promote Amelia's happiness more ways than one.

L. Fal. Then I am the veriest wretch that ever exifted.—But take her, Sir! for I muft confefs that you have deferved her by your proceedings; and that I, fool and villain that I was, have forfeited her by mine. *[Going.*

Free. Hold, hold! one word before you go, if you pleafe, my lord! You may kill yourfelf for aught I know, but you fha'n't lay your death at my door, I promife you. I had a kindnefs for Amelia, I muft confefs; but in the courfe of my late negotiation for Sir William, hearing of your lordfhip's pretenfions, I dropt all thoughts of her. It is a maxim with me, to do good wherever I can, but always to abftain from doing mifchief.— Now as I can't make the lady happy myfelf, I would fain put her into the hands of thofe that can.—So, if you would oblige me, Sir William, let me join thefe two young folks together, *[joining their hands]* and do you fay Amen to it.

Sir Will. With all my heart!—You can have no objection, Amelia. *[Amelia burfts into tears.*

L. Fal. How bitterly do thofe tears reproach me! It fhall be the whole bufinefs of my future life to atone for them.

H 2   *Amelia.*

Amelia. Your actions this day, and your folicitude for my father, have redeemed you in my good opinion ! and the confent of Sir William, feconded by fo powerful an advocate as Mr. Freeport, cannot be contended with. Take my hand, my lord ! a virtuous paffion may inhabit the pureft breaft ; and I am not afhamed to confefs, that I had conceived a partiality for you, till your own conduct turned my heart againft you ; and if my refentment has given you any pain, when I confider the occafion, I muft own that I cannot repent it.

L. Fal. Mention it no more, my love, I befeech you ! You may juftly blame your lover, I confefs ; but I will never give you caufe to complain of your hufband.

Free. I don't believe you will. I give you joy, my lord ; I give you all joy ! As for you, madam, [*to Amelia.*] do but fhew the world that you can bear profperity, as well as you have fuftained the fhocks of adverfity, and there are few women, who may not wifh to be an Amelia.

E P I-

Enter lady Alton in a paffion; Spatter following.

Lady Alton.

I'LL hear no more, thou wretch !—Attend to
    reafon !
A woman of my rank !—'Tis petty treafon !
Hear reafon, blockhead ! Reafon ! What is that ?
Bid me wear pattens, and a high-crown'd hat !
Won't you be gone ?—what want you ?—what's
    your view ?

Spatter.

Humbly to ferve the Tuneful Nine in you.————
I muft invoke you————

Lady Alton.

        I renounce fuch things ;
Not Phœbus now, but vengeance fweeps the ftrings ;
My mind is difcord all !—I fcorn, deteft
All human kind !—*you* more than all the reft.

Spatter.

I humbly thank you, ma'am.—But weigh the matter,

Lady Alton.

I won't hear reafon ! and I hate you, Spatter !
Myfelf, and ev'ry thing————

H 3

Spatter.

Spatter.

That I deny;
You love a little mifchief; fo do I;
And mifchief I have for you.——

Lady Alton.

How, where, when?
Will you ftab Falbridge?

Spatter.

Yes, ma'am—with my pen.

Lady Alton.

Let loofe, my Spatter, till to death you've ftung'em,
That green-ey'd monfter Jealoufy, among 'em.

Spatter.

To dafh at all, the fpirit of my trade is,
Men, women, children, parfons, lords and ladies.——
There will be danger.

Lady Alton.

And there fhall be pay.
Take my purfe, Spatter!   [*Gives it him.*

Spatter.   [*Smiles and takes it.*

In an honeft way.

Lady Alton.

Should my lord beat you——

Spatter.

Let them laugh that win!
For all my bruifes, here's *gold-beater's fkin.*

[*Chinking the purfe.*
                                                Lady

EPILOGUE.

Lady Alton.

Nay, fhould he kill you——

Spatter.

Ma'am!

Lady Alton.

My kindnefs meant,

To pay your merit with a monument.

Spatter.

Your kindnefs, lady, takes away my breath;
We'll ftop, with your good leave, on this fide death.

Lady Alton.

Attack Amelia, both in verfe and profe:
Your wit can make a nettle of a rofe.

Spatter.

A ftinging-nettle for his lordfhip's breaft;
And to my *ftars* and *dafhes* leave the reft.
I'll make 'em miferable, never fear;
Pout in a month, and part in half a year.
I know my genius, and can truft my plan;
I'll break a woman's heart with any man.

Lady Alton.

Thanks, thanks, dear Spatter! be fevere, and bold!

Spatter.

No qualms of confcience with a purfe of gold;
Tho' pill'ries threaten, and tho' crabfticks fall,
Yours are my heart, foul, pen, ears, bones, and all.

[*Exit Spatter.*

Lady

EPILOGUE.

Lady Alton alone.

Thus to the winds at once my cares I scatter——
Oh, 'tis a charming rascal, this same Spatter !
His precious mischief makes the storm subside !
My anger, thank my stars ! all rose from pride.
Pride should belong to us alone of fashion ;
And let the mob take love, that vulgar passion !
Love, pity, tenderness, are only made
For poets, Abigails, and folks in trade ;
Some cits about their *feelings* make a fuss,
And some are better bred—who live with us ;
How low lord Falbridge is !—He takes a wife,
To love, and cherish, and be fix'd for life !
Thinks marriage is a *comfortable* state,
No pleasure like a *vartuous téte-à-téte !*
Do our lords justice, for I would not wrong 'em,
There are not many such poor souls among 'em.
Our turtles from the town will fly with speed,
And I'll foretell the vulgar life they'll lead.
With love and ease grown fat, they face all weather,
And, farmers both, trudge arm in arm together:
Now view their stock, now in their nurs'ry prattle,
For ever with their children, or their cattle.
Like the dull mill-horse in one round they keep ;
They walk, talk, fondle, dine, and fall asleep ;
Their custom always in the afternoon——
He bright as *Sol,* and she *the chaste full-moon !*

Wak'd

EPILOGUE.

Wak'd with their coffee, madam firſt begins,
She rubs her eyes, his lordſhip rubs his ſhins;
She ſips, and ſmirks;—"Next week's our wedding-
 "day,
"Married ſeven years!—And ev'ry hour *(yawns)*
 "more gay!"
"True, Emmy, (cries my lord)—the bleſſing lies,
"Our hearts in ev'ry thing *(yawns)* ſo ſympathize!
The day thus ſpent, my lord for muſick calls;
He thrums the baſs, to which my lady ſqualls;
The children join, which ſo delights theſe ninnies,
The brats ſeem all *Guarduccis—Lovatinis.*
—What means this qualm?—Why, ſure, while
 I'm deſpiſing,
That vulgar paſſion Envy, is not riſing!
Oh, no!—Contempt is ſtruggling to burſt out:
I'll give it vent at lady Scalp'em's *route.*

THE

MAN OF BUSINESS,

A

COMEDY.

First acted at the Theatre-Royal in Covent-Garden, on the 29th of January, 1774.

——*Mihi res, non me rebus submittere conor.* Hor.

TO THE HONOURABLE

CONSTANTINE JOHN PHIPPS.

SIR,

WERE the motives of dedication candidly acknowledged, perhaps it would appear that authors in general rather intend a compliment to their own vanity, than to that of their patrons. Patron, I flatter myself, will, in the prefent inftance, appear to you too cold and diftant an expreffion; and though I entertain all due refpect for fuperior rank and fituation, and am happy in feizing an opportunity of declaring to the world that I am honoured with the friendfhip of Mr. Phipps, yet never was there an epiftle of this nature, in which mere vanity had a more inconfiderable fhare; nor fhould I be thus proud of proclaiming my affection for him, were I not convinced of his being poffeffed of qualities and accomplifhments that would diftinguifh and adorn the moft humble, as well as the moft elevated fituation.

In

DEDICATION.

In the midst of the most familiar intercourse, I should be loth to forfeit in any degree the partiality you are pleased to shew me, by the smallest appearance of flattery. But when I do but echo the voice of all those who are acquainted with your publick or private character; when I barely observe, that in an age of the most unbounded dissipation, you have devoted your time to the attainment of all useful and elegant knowledge; joining to the most amiable disposition the most unshaken integrity, as well as a thorough acquaintance with the constitution of your country, together with the most able and faithful discharge of the duties of your profession—when I just faintly sketch these outlines of your character, it will, I hope, rather be supposed that I presume to hint to you what the world seems to expect from a young man of fashion of so great promise, than that I mean to corrupt you, or degrade myself, by idle compliment and mean adulation.

Of the Comedy which I now present to you, I will venture to say but little. It is difficult for any man to speak with a tolerable grace of himself, and literary performances ought to be their own recommendation; yet I will not scruple to confess, that if I thought it entirely despicable, I would not

solicit

folicit your acceptance of it. Three of the great writers, enumerated in the Prologue, Plautus, Terence, and Marmontel, have contributed to enrich it. A play lately exhibited on the French ftage, the Deux Amis of M. Beaumarchais, alfo fuggefted fome hints of the fable; but the traces of them in this Comedy are fo little apparent, that if I did not thus acknowledge the fources from which I have drawn, I queftion if the ingenious author himfelf would be able to claim his own property.

Did I conceive that this play contained any paffages unfavourable to liberty, more efpecially the liberty of the prefs, you, Sir, would be one of the laft perfons in the kingdom to whofe protection I fhould venture to recommend it. The liberty of the prefs is a moft invaluable privilege; yet that liberty, like every other fpecies of liberty, may be abufed; and while it remains (as it is to be hoped it ever will remain) unreftrained by law, the abufe of it is more peculiarly the object of comedy; whofe province it is, by wholefome and general fatire, to correct thofe failings and enormities, of which the law takes no cognifance. Better were it that thoufands and ten thoufands of fuch infignificant

nificant individuals as myfelf fhould be malicioufly
flandered, than that facred right of Englifhmen
fhould be violated or infringed: Yet who will juf-
tify the fcandalous perfonalities (politicks entirely
out of the queftion) that difgrace our newfpapers?
It is not however fufficient, it feems, to endure
them patiently, without a wifh to interrupt their
progrefs, but the gentleft retort is enough to fet
all Grub-ftreet in an uproar; and the moft good-
humoured ridicule of thefe illuftrious authors is an
attack upon the liberty of the prefs!—A liberty
which they are zealous to exercife in its fulleft ex-
tent, without allowing any portion of it to their
opponents; not confidering that the chief benefit
of the liberty of the prefs refults from its being
open to all, and affording a free examination of
both fides of every queftion. The very liberty
they take, however, they are not willing to give;
like a fcavenger I faw the other day in the ftreet,
who befpattered every paffenger with the contents
of his mud-cart, but fent a volley of curfes after
a lady of quality, who happened to fplafh him as
fhe drove by in her chariot.

Having faid thus much of my Comedy, in vin-
dication of the freedom I have ufed in infcribing

it

DEDICATION.

it to you, I will not trefpafs longer on your patience, than to repeat the fatisfaction I feel in thus
openly teftifying my regard; and that I have the
honour to be,

Sir,

Your moft devoted, faithful,

And affectionate humble Servant,

GEORGE COLMAN.

PROLOGUE.

Spoken by Mr. WOODWARD.

Enter as an Author, with a manuscript.

SEE here, good folks, how genius is abus'd!
A play of mine, the manager refus'd!
And why?—I knew the reaſon well enough——
Only to introduce his own damn'd ſtuff.
Oh! he's an arrogant, invidious elf,
Who hates all wit, and has no wit himſelf!
As to the plays on which he builds his fame,
Boaſting your praiſe, *we all know whence they came.*
Crown him with ivy, leaſt of Brentford kings!
For ſtill, like ivy, round ſome oak he clings.
Plays you have damn'd, their authors yet unknown,
Truſt me, good people, thoſe were all his own.
If his lame genius ever ſtood the teſt,
"Twas but a crutch'd noun adjective at beſt;
Or rather *expletive*, whoſe weak pretence
Occupies ſpace, but adds not to the ſenſe.
His lady-muſe, tho' puling, wan, and thin,
With green-room caudle all in ſtate lies-in;
His brats ſo ricketty, 'tis ſtill their curſe
To be ſwath'd, ſwaddled, and put out to nurſe;

Brought

PROLOGUE.

Brought up on playhouse pap, they waule and cry,
Crawl on the stage, or in convulsions die.

His play to-night, like all he ever wrote,
Is pie-ball'd, piec'd, and patch'd, like Joseph's coat;
Made up of shreds from Plautus and Corneille,
Terence, Moliere, Voltaire, and Marmontel;
With rags from fifty others I might mention,
Which proves him dull and barren of invention:
But shall his nonsense hold the place of sense?
No, damn him! damn him, in your own defence!
Else on your mercy will the dwarf presume,
Nor e'er give giant Genius elbow-room.

Now, now, my friends, we've brought him to the
      stake;
Bait him! and then, perhaps, some sport he'll make.
I've lin'd the house in front, above, below;
Friends, like dried figs, stuck close in every row!
Some wits in ambush, in the gallery sit;
Some form a critick phalanx in the pit;
Some scatter'd forces their shrill catcalls play,
And strike the Tiny Scribbler with dismay.
On then, my hearts! charge! fire! your triumph's
      certain
O'er his weak battery from behind the curtain!
To-morrow's Chronicle your deeds shall boast,
And loud *Te Deums* fill the Morning-Post.

     DRAMATIS

DRAMATIS PERSONÆ.

FABLE,	Mr. Bensley.
GOLDING,	Mr. Shuter.
BEVERLEY,	Mr. Lewis.
DENIER,	Mr. Lewes.
TROPICK,	Mr. Woodward.
CHECK,	Mr. Quick.
HANDY,	Mr. Dyer.
Lord RIOT,	Mr. Davis.
Sir HELTER SKELTER,	Mr. Fox.
Colonel RAKISH,	Mr. Owenson.
SCANTY,	Mr. Gardner.
CAPIAS,	Mr. Kniveton.
SNAP,	Mr. Thompson.
HAZARD,	Mr. Cushing.
CASH,	Mr. Hamilton.
Servant,	Mr. Bates.
Mrs. GOLDING,	Mrs. Green.
LYDIA,	Mrs. Bulkley.
Mrs. CARLTON,	Mrs. Pitt.
Mrs. FLOUNCE,	Mrs. Helme.

THE

THE

MAN OF BUSINESS.

ACT I.

An apartment in Golding's house.

Enter Fable and Mrs. Golding.

(She in a fancy dress, with a mask in her hand.)

Fable.

MADAM, madam, I tell you he is a cox-comb—an arrant coxcomb, Mrs. Golding.

Mrs. Gold. He is a gentleman—thoroughly the gentleman, Mr. Fable.

Fable. Yes, a modern gentleman—a fine gentle-man—a race of puppies more pernicious to this country than a breed of wolves would have been. —A mongrel puppy too; on a wrong scent after pleasure; in chase of the fashion, but for ever at fault; with vanity in view, and ridicule for a whipper-in.

Mrs. Gold. Well, well, Mr. Fable, it does not

signify

fignify talking. You know, you and I could never agree on this matter. I was always for my kinf-man's keeping the very beft company; and, for my part, I fee no great difference between him and his friends of quality—Nay, indeed, mongrel, as you are pleafed to call him, Sir, the advantage is rather on his fide : He has money without rank, and many of them have rank without money. If Beverley has great goings-out, he has great com-ing-in too; while they keep fine houfes, flaming equipages, and great tables, out of nothing at all.

Fable. For which very reafon, Mrs. Golding, he is not upon even terms with them. What has a man of bufinefs to do with men of pleafure? Why is a young banker to live with young no-blemen ?

Mrs. Gold. And why not, Mr. Fable ? Is not the bufinefs of the houfe carried on at the polite end of the town ? Does not he live in the very centre of perfons of fafhion ? And has not he conftant dealings with them ?—Not fhut up in Lombard-ftreet—within the found of Bow-bell, or in fight of the Monument—not cramming turtle and venifon at the King's Arms, or the London-Tavern—but balloted into the Macaroni, and a member of the Sçavoir Vivre.

Fable. So much the worfe—fo much the worfe,
Mrs.

Mrs. Golding! His father, who was the firm of the house, eftablished the credit of it by decency and fobriety: But dying while Beverley was very young, your hufband, Mr. Golding, was received into the partnerfhip as a man of experience, capable of carrying on the bufinefs to more advantage. He, you know, is now abfent on neceffary bufinefs abroad. In the mean time, I am left a kind of guardian to Beverley, and have the fuperintendance of his affairs—And what account fhall I be likely to give of them, when inftead of making money after the example of his father, he is intent on nothing but fpending it? Horfes at Newmarket, hounds at Bagfhot, a villa, a miftrefs, play, and a round of diffipation among hair-brain'd fpendthrifts, wafting their conftitutions before they arrive at maturity, fpending their fortunes before they come to them, granting annuities to eat up their eftates, or living upon the fale of poft-obits and reverfions!—There, madam, there's a picture of a genteel young banker at the weft-end of the town for you; drawn from the life, and coloured after nature! how do you like it, madam?

Mrs. Gold. A frightful caricature, Mr. Fable! your defcriptions are juft the reverfe of that fweet

I 4   flower

flower of a man, the auctioneer, over the way. His ftile is enchanting and delicate, elegant as the *or moulu*, or Derbyfhire petrifications, he fets to fale, and foft as the pencil of Guido, Raphael, or Correggio! Your pictures may be taken from nature; but they are dark!—dark as the landfcapes of Pouffin, and wild, and horrible as the views of Salvator Rofa.

Fable. Madam, madam! it is thefe affected airs, madam, that pervert your underftanding, and make you blind to the danger of your kinfman.— He is in imminent danger of ruin, madam; which will fall upon him, if fomething is not fpeedily done to prevent it.

Mrs. Gold. And what would you have me do, Mr. Fable? All I fay is, that good company is a very good thing, and genteel connections can never do my kinfman any mifchief; and if I had been miftrefs, I never would have refted till I had got him into parliament.

Fable. Into parliament!—into jail, madam. Is not he at expence enough——

Mrs. Gold. Expence! Lord, lord! this is a point of œconomy, Sir. Why he would fave above double the charge of bringing him into the houfe by the mere poftage of letters.—Sir Geoffry Kil-

derkin

derkin got himfelf elected for no other purpofe.—
My kinfman too would frank himfelf whole again.
—And then I am fure he would make an admirable figure in a debate.—Oh, how it would have
delighted me to have fat among the ladies in the
gallery of the houfe—to have feen him upon his
feet, his whole perfon hanging over his right leg,
his right arm fwinging to and fro like a pen-
dulum, and his tongue running down like a
larum !

Fable. So, fo ! you, I fear, are too far gone for
wholefome counfel. Beverley, I hope, is not quite
incorrigible, and fome good may be done upon
him. Good morrow to you, madam ! I have bufinefs. Good day, madam.

Mrs. Gold. Good night, if you pleafe, Sir. You
may be juft up, but I have not been to bed yet,
being (as you fee) but juft come from the Pantheon.
The mafquerade began to grow thin ; but my kinfman, who was there, is not come home yet, and
may not return for fome time perhaps—fo, once
more, good night, good Mr. Fable ! I'll endeavour
to recruit my fpirits from the fatigue of the pleafures of the night, and leave you to the bufinefs
of the day. Your fervant, Sir. [*Exit.*

Fable

Fable alone.

Your fervant, madam!—A weak woman! incapable indeed of fwaying the mind of Beverley by her advice, but ftill ferving to countenance his follies by her example. But now to the bufinefs of the day, as fhe fays!—A ferious day it will appear to the young gentleman, I fancy. But it is high time to make him ferious. I'll juft allow him a fhort interval to fleep off his mafquerade, and then wake him from his dream of folly to a fenfe of his true fituation.

Enter Check.

Fable. Good morrow, Check!

Check. Good morrow to your honour! The fhop is juft opened and fprinkled. I am going to the counting-houfe.

Fable. That's right, Check. Regularity and punctuality are the life of bufinefs.

Check. The life and foul, Sir. I have always found them fo. Always exact myfelf, I can anfwer —always precife to a fecond! and as true to my time as the men that ftrike the quarters at St. Dunftan's. Ha, ha!

Fable. You're merry, Check!

Check. Ah! I wifh I had caufe, Sir. Another
great

·great houfe in the city ftopt payment yefterday, and a large fum fubfcribed to prop the credit of another. Sad times, Mr. Fable!

Fable. Sad times! fad men, honeft Check. Men make the times.

Check. Very true, very true, Sir. Ah, one need not go far from home to know that, Sir. In poor old Mr. Beverley's time, when we carried on bufinefs in Threadneedle-ftreet, thofe were days, Mr. Fable! I wifh we were on the other fide of Temple-bar, again!

Fable. No, no; you are right juft where you are, friend. The two fides of Temple-bar have changed hands, Check. The gay, fmart, airy fparks of the weft-end of the town, have all taken to bufinefs, and are turned fheriffs and aldermen; and the merchants, bankers, and tradefmen, are your principal perfons of pleafure now-a-days.

Check. Ah, I am afraid fo. Here's a houfe, forfooth! my old lady always entertaining company at home, and my young mafter always abroad; night turned into day, and day turned into night! It was not fo in my old mafter's time. Never out of the regular channel; fure and moderate profit; quiet, fober living; a plain joint and a pudding on week-days, and, perhaps, two joints and two puddings on Sunday!

Fable.

Fable. Nay, nay, don't be melancholy, Check. You may live to fee two puddings on table again, perhaps.

Check. We have no hopes but in you, Mr. Fable; no hope but in you, Sir! Every thing would go to wreck and ruin, if it was not for you, Sir.

Fable. Come, come; cheer up, honeſt Check! your young maſter will take up ſhortly. He has a good heart, and a good underſtanding.

Check. I wiſh he would make lefs uſe of his heart, and more of his underſtanding, Sir. He is as generous as a prince, and he thinks all his acquaintance as honeſt and generous as himſelf. Let him mind his friend, Mr. Denier, Sir. There's a young man for you! merry and wiſe, I warrant him! He knows that a ſhilling is a ſerious thing; that a penny ſaved is a penny got; and two and two make four, Sir.

Fable. Beverley will find it out at laſt, Check.— Have you prepared the books and papers as I directed you?

Check. I have, Sir.

Fable. Very well. Let them be ready for inſpection this very morning; and tell Mr. Beverley I am gone to the Bank; but deſire he would not be out of the way at my return, as I have ſome-

thing

thing of confequence to fay to him. Good morrow, Check!

Check. Good morrow to your honour! I fhall
be fure to let Mr. Beverley know, Sir.

[*Exit Fable.*

Oh, here comes his *gentleman,* as they call him.
wifh there was not fuch a gentleman within the
bills of mortality.

Enter Handy.

Good morrow to you, Mr. Handy! Good morrow!

Handy. What! my old Rule of Three! are you
there? Good morrow to you!

Check. Mr. Beverley is not up yet, I fuppofe.

Handy. Then you fuppofe wrong, old Thread-
needle! He is up, I affure you.

Check. Indeed! why he is more early than ordinary, Mr. Handy.

Handy. Much later than ordinary, mafter Check.
He has not been to bed yet.

Check. Mercy on me! paft eight in the morning, and not gone to bed yet!

Handy. No, he's not come home from the mafquerade.

Check. The mafquerade! Oh, now you have
accounted for it.

Handy.

Handy. Yes, I had fome thoughts of being at the Pantheon myfelf; but——

Check. What! at the fixpenny Pantheon at Iflington, Mr. Handy?

Handy. Sixpenny Pantheon! 'Sdeath, what d'ye mean, Sir? do ye take me for a little fhop-keeping mechanick, or one of your dapper city clerks, that draws his pen from under his ear in the evening, to go and drink tea at Bagnigge-Wells or Dobney's Bowling-Green? No, Sir; let me tell you, I frequent no diverfions but thofe of perfons of quality. Plays now and then, operas twice a week, and mafquerades whenever there are any.——A lady of my particular acquaintance—of the firft fafhion I affure you, old gentleman,—had provided me a ticket, and a domino, with a fmart hat and feather, and diamond button and loop to it.——But, as the devil would have it, my lord du——zounds, what was I faying?——Her hufband, I fay, happening to come in at an unfortunate moment, faw the drefs lying in her apartment. My lady—a devilifh clever woman, upon my foul! turned it off with a laugh, and told him fhe had provided them on purpofe for him, in order to furprife him with a piece of conjugal gallantry. So away they went to the Pantheon together, and I was obliged to amufe myfelf with another woman of quality, who kept

houfe

houfe all the evening, to confole myfelf for my difappointment.

Check. You imagine I have a large portion of faith, I believe, Mr. Handy.

Handy. Faith!—Why, have I offered to borrow any money of you, you old multiplication-table? Eh?.

Check. You have not taken that liberty with me, becaufe you knew I would lend you none: but you are rather too familiar with your betters, me-thinks.

Handy. They are familiar with us, and encourage. familiarities on our fide.—Nay, if you would fol-low my advice, I would engage to make a fortune even for you, old Methufalem!

Check. For me, Mr. Handy?

Handy. Ay, for you, old boy! What do you think now of making love to Mrs. Golding? Her hufband's abroad, you know. Intrigues are the mode, and fhe loves to be in the fafhion.—Devil take me, if I don't think fhe and you would make an excellent *tête-à-tête.*—Shalum and Hilpa! Eh, my old antediluvian?

Check. A truce with your wit, good Mr. Handy! and pleafe to let your mafter know, that Mr. Fable defires to fee him on fome particular bufinefs, as

foon

foon as he is ftirring,—which, perhaps, may be about dinner-time.

Handy. What! Do you pretend to joke too? Pounds, fhillings, and pence,—you had beft ftick to that, old gentleman.

Check. They won't ftick to you long; I am afraid, young gentleman. Ha, ha!

Handy. Again! You are trying to copy after old mafter Fable, I warrant you.—A fly, dry, queer old buck, that Mr. Fable! He don't much approve of our proceedings, I believe. The people call my mafter the Macaroni Banker, he fays. [*Laugh heard*] —Gadfo! yonder my mafter comes, faith———— and along with him his bofom friend, Mr. Denier —a fnake in his bofom too, if I am not miftaken. I never could endure that fhrewd fpark fince I heard him upon the chapter of vails—which he never gives to other peoples' fervants; but, for fear of raifing the wages at home, fuffers them to be taken by his own. A young curmudgeon! worfe than a liquorifh old dotard, if poffible. What fay you, Grandfire?—[*laugh again*]—But, hufh, they are here.—Now you may deliver your errand to him yourfelf, old gentleman.

[*Check and Handy retire a little.*

Enter

*Enter Beverley and Denier. (Beverley in a domino ;
Denier alfo in a mafquerade drefs.)*

Bev. Support a character at a mafquerade! Abfurd and ridiculous! and a vulgar idea too, that
never entered the head of a gentleman.

Denier. Oh, my habit gave me no trouble of
that fort; yet I did not wear it from choice, but
from convenience. One of the managers of Covent-Garden theatre—for there are about five and
forty of them, you know—lent me the drefs; and
I don't fee why I fhould be expected to fupport a
character in it any more than thofe who ufually
wear it.—Eh, Beverley?

Bev. No, to be fure. They who fay the fofteft
things, and fucceed moft with the women, enter
into the fpirit and genius of the place the moft
happily. Gallantry and intrigue, not wit and humour, are the objects of a mafquerade.

Denier. I beg your pardon, Beverley. I know
more than one or two profeffed jokers, that re-
hearfe their parts for a fortnight before-hand, and
write down all the good things they fhall fay;
but, as ill luck will have it, for want of courage
and opportunity, never utter one of them; and yet,
refolving they fhall not be loft to the world, fend
them, ready cut and dry, to the news-papers, as

having been their extempore fallies and mafquerade pleafantries.

Bev. Oh, I know the little haberdafhers of fmall wit; I know them, Denier, and thank you for your defcription of them.—But who the deuce was that very elegant-looking woman that lord Robert Sprightly ftuck fo clofe to for moft part of the evening? I have a ftrong notion it was lady Sarah Brilliant—very like her figure! or Harriot Freelove—but her—fhe's common, you know—her he would not have followed fo warmly.—Oh, Check, are you there?—Handy too? [*Check and Handy come forward.*] Have you fet my night-things in my bed-chamber?

Handy. They are all ready, Sir.

Bev. Did you prefent Sir John Squanderfield's notes for acceptance, Check?

Check. I did, Sir.

Bev. Any cards, Handy?—And were they good bills, Check?

Handy. The cards, tickets, and meffages lie on your dreffing-table, Sir.

Bev. Very well.—And were Sir John's notes duly accepted, Check?

Check. They ought to have been duly *protefted*, Sir.—Not good bills—not worth a farthing, Sir.—I have not given him credit for them.

Bev-

Bev. Well, let him have due notice, d'ye hear, Check?—And do you call at the *Sçavoir,* and let them know that I fhall dine there to-day, d'ye hear, Handy?—And do you come to me with the ftate of Sir John's account, as foon as I am up, d'ye hear, Check?

Check. The account is ready, Sir; but Mr. Fable defires to fpeak with you as foon as you are up, Sir. He is gone into the city, but will return before you are ftirring, and has particular bufinefs.

Bev. I fhall be ready to attend him. Let me be called about one, d'ye hear, Handy?—I have nothing further to fay to you at prefent, Check.

Check. Mighty well, Sir.

Bev. Handy, wait in my chamber.

Handy. I fhall, Sir.

[*Exeunt Check and Handy feverally.*

Manent Beverley and Denier.

Bev. You'll dine with us at the *Sçavoir,* Denier?

Denier. That's impoffible. Lady Quaver, who fubfcribes to the opera, has lent her box to Mrs. Carlton and Lydia this evening, and I have promifed to attend them; fo we muft make a fhort early dinner at home. You will hardly rife from table before the *finale.*

Bev.

Bev. Time enough to fee the Heinel walk over the courfe, perhaps: but the places of publick diverfion do keep moft diforderly hours, to be fure. As to the play-houfes, I fcarce ever attempt to peep into them. There is no getting a mouthful of tragedy or comedy, without balking one's appetite for every thing elfe. But Lydia is fond of plays too; and the little prude is fo eager and punctual, fhe is as fure to be at the drawing-up of the curtain as if fhe went to keep places.

Denier. Come, come, after all, you are very partial to my ward, Beverley. She is fevere upon your gaiety, and you rally her prudery. You both think it worth while to find fault with each other; and that's a dreadful fymptom, Beverley.

Bev. No, no; not fo far gone as that neither. —The girl has fome good natural qualities; but fhe has not mixed with the world enough.—She is like one of our Englifh coaches—made of good ftuff, and not ill fafhion'd—but wants the high Paris varnifh, Denier.

Denier. I have a good mind to acquaint her with your comparifon.—She'll varnifh you till you appear like lord Rufty's pictures—not much the better for it.——But, apropos to your fimile,— after your coach has fet you down to dinner in St.

James's

James's Street, can you fend it to carry us to the opera?

Bev. To be fure. They are not put up yet. I'll give orders about it immediately.

Denier. Stay! Suppofe it takes me home then; and I'll tell them your direction.—I fhall hardly get a chair at this time in the morning.

Bev. Be it fo. Good night to you.—But, Denier!

Denier. Well.

Bev. There is to be another mafquerade next week, at the Haymarket. Will you go?

Denier. No—hang it; next week is too foon for it.—So much of it makes it grow naufeous.

Bev. It will be a genteel thing.

Denier. A genteel mafquerade?—Oh, that's the devil, Beverley. The company at a mafquerade fhould be almoft as various as the characters they reprefent.—Countefles and fempftreffes, lords, aldermen, black-legs, and Oxonians.—Make your mafquerade too genteel, and it muft be very dull, Beverley.

Bev. All the fine women in town will be there. It is to be given by the club at Arthur's. I can fupply you with tickets.

Denier. Can you?—Well then—come, for once, I will go with you.

K 3

Bev.

Bev. Now, if you could prevail on Lydia to go too——

Denier. No; she won't take the Paris varnish, Beverley.

Bev. I am forry for it. Then there's no hopes of her.

Denier. Poor Beverley! Adieu!

Bev. Poor Lydia, I fay. I'll go to-bed, and dream of her reformation. Good night to you.

[Exeunt feverally.

A C T II,

Beverley's dreffing-room. A writing-defk and dreffing-table, chairs, &c.

Bell rings two or three times violently; at length enter Handy, in a morning drefs, rubbing his eyes.

Handy.

RING, ring, ring! The devil's in Mr. Beverley to-day, I think. He defires to be waked about one or two, and is ready to pull the bells out of the pullies between eleven and twelve. [*Rings.*] Again! I'll be with you in a moment, Sir. [*Yawns.*]

If

If he had been at deep play laſt night, I ſhould have
thought his loſſes had diſturbed him—or, if he had
been drinking, that his reſt was ſpoil'd with ſick-
neſs and head-ache.—But to come home ſober, and
in good humour, and then drag one out of bed like
a ſchool-boy, or an apprentice—[*Rings again.*]
Well, well, I am coming—Stay till I can get to
you, Sir. [*Going.*] Not he, faith—here he is—
walking in his ſleep, for aught I know—for I am
ſure, I am hardly awake yet.   [*Yawning.*

Enter Beverley.

Bev. Oh, you are here, I ſee. I thought you
were dead, Handy.

Handy. Dead aſleep, Sir. I had hardly got warm
in bed, in my firſt doze, Sir.   [*Yawning.*

Bev. Come, come, my breakfaſt! I have no
time for dozing and dreaming. To keep my en-
gagements at night, I muſt diſpatch a good deal
of buſineſs in the morning. [*Sits.*] Reach me that
bundle of papers. [*Handy brings them from the deſk.*]
I muſt anſwer theſe letters. Now chocolate, Handy;
chocolate immediately!

Handy. [*Aſide.*] Whew!   [*Exit yawning.*

Bev. [*Untying the bundle.*] Say what they will
of your dull fellows and drudges, men of ſpirit are

your only perfons of difpatch—diligent in their bufinefs for the fake of getting rid of it—not working flowly, grub, grub, like a mole, but ftraining to the goal like a racer.—Let me fee, what have we here? [*Looking at one of the letters.*] Oh, a letter from Mr. Golding's old Quaker friend and correfpondent, Ephraim Quiet of Briftol.

Re-enter Handy.

Handy. The chocolate, Sir.

Bev. Very well—Set it down, Handy—and tell Check to come to me with the account I fpoke to him about, when I came home laft night.

Handy. He's here already, Sir, and Mr. Fable too.

Enter Fable, attended by Check, with books and papers.

Bev. [*Rifing.*] Mr. Fable, your very humble fervant.

Fable. Oh, your fervant, your fervant.—Are you fure you have all the books and papers with you, Check?

Check. Very fure, Sir.

Fable. And have you the inftrument from my attorney?

Check. It is here, Sir.

Fable. And the balances of the feveral accounts are all right and exact?

Check.

Check. To the fixteenth of a farthing, Sir; I have proved them again and again, Sir.

Fable. Very well. Lay them on the table then. I fhall be with you prefently in the counting-houfe.

Check. You will be fure to find me there, Sir.

[*Lays down books, &c. and exit.*

Fable. And now indulge me with a word or two in private, Mr. Beverley.

Bev. Pray be feated, Sir. Handy, wait in the antichamber.

Handy. I fhall, Sir. [*Exit.*

Manent Fable and Beverley, fitting.

Fable. [*After a fhort paufe.*] I am afraid I have broken in upon you rather abruptly, Mr. Beverley.

Bev. Not at all, Sir.

Fable. My bufinefs is preffing, and I muft be as abrupt in difclofing it.

Bev. Pray what is it, Sir?

Fable. I fhould wifh to adminifter comfort, rather than to diftrefs or furprife you; but there is no time for delicacies, or room for palliation.

Bev. You amaze me! What do you mean, Sir?

Fable. Don't be too much alarmed neither; don't let it totally difcourage you. You are young, you know——

Bev.

Bev. Relieve me from fufpenfe, I befeech you, Sir.

Fable. Nay, I can't fay it is downright ruin neither.

Bev. Ruin, Mr. Fable!

Fable. No; not abfolutely. Your credit and character may be both a little fhaken by it at firft, indeed; but, with induftry, thank Heaven, you will have time and opportunity to re-eftablifh them.

Bev. You keep me on the rack! Let me comprehend you. Be plain, Sir!

Fable. In a word then—what do you think of the failure of the houfe?

Bev. Sir!

Fable. Stopping payment?

Bev. Impoffible!

Fable. Ten days ago I was of your opinion.—But thofe papers, Mr. Beverley, among which are copies of the laft letters from Mr. Golding, will convince you that the danger is imminent.

Bev. Why, why was I not more early apprifed of this, Mr. Fable?

Fable. You have a great deal on your hands, you know; and I did not care to interrupt your amufements, or damp your vivacity, till I had examined and fettled the ftate of your affairs. I was in

hopes,

hopes, indeed, matters had not been fo defperate. —But one misfortune is always accompanied by another, and another followed by more.—'The infurance not being done on the Speedwell and Thetis, owing to the mifcarriage of Mr. Golding's letters from Bengal; the wreck of both thofe Indiamen, as well as Mr. Golding's other loffes in India; the failure of the houfes at Amfterdam; the late run upon our own; and the bills we have accepted being fo foon payable—are unlucky circumftances, all concurring to perplex and embarras us.

Bev. And what—what's to be done then, Mr. Fable ?

Fable. Oh, don't be too uneafy! the fhock is rather violent and fudden, to be fure; but I hope to extricate you with honour and reputation.

Bev. You revive me. By what means, Sir?

Fable. When you have look'd into the vouchers which Check has left with you, you will fee the neceffity of executing this inftrument, conftituting me your fole truftee and creditor; I having undertaken to fatisfy every other claim and demand upon the houfe.—All that concerns me is, that, in order to come handfomely through this bufinefs, and to appear in earneft to the world, we muft exact fome co-operation on your part, fome little facrifices from you, Mr. Beverley.

Bev.

Bev. Sacrifices from me! what facrifices, Mr. Fable?

Fable. Not that I think they will affect you much, neither. I was happy, to be fure, to fee you keeping the very beft company, making a figure on the turf, regularly attending the hunt, and entertaining handfomely both here, and at Wimbledon.—But people in bufinefs are liable to thefe accidents— and pleafure, you know, muft give way when preffing exigencies require it. Put your horfes to fale, part with your hounds, fell your villa—and as a narrower plan of living, a fyftem of œconomy, will render all the plate and prefent furniture unneceffary, I think it will be advifeable to lett this houfe too. A fmaller will ferve to carry on the bufinefs.

Bev. Sell my horfes and hounds! part with my houfes! difpofe of my plate, Mr. Fable! furely this is being rather too precipitate. It fhould be very maturely confidered, whether we cannot fmother thefe evils, without letting them burft into a flame immediately.

Fable. That has been thoroughly confidered, depend upon't—nay, I have already convened the capital creditors, and convinced them of the certainty of their demands being fatisfied, on the plan I have propofed to you. They are perfuaded that

the

the houſe will ultimately prove good and ſufficient, and have engaged to ſupport it. Some few indeed ſeemed to doubt your concurrence and perſeverance; but I (who think I know you better) undertook to anſwer for both. The truth is, you have no alternative.—The affair is publick by this time,, and the eyes of the whole world are upon you.—But, courage, Beverley! you have youth, as I told you, and honour, and abilities: They are now put to the teſt, and I have no fear of your conduct. When you have finiſhed your breakfaſt, run your eye over the account, read Mr. Golding's laſt letters, examine the deed of truſt, and conſider what I have ſaid to you. Your ſervant! Good day to you! Your ſervant!   [*Exit.*

Beverley alone.

What is all this? Veſſels uninſured! Failure of correſpondents! Letters from Mr. Golding! Loſſes in India! Sure our ſituation cannot be ſo bad as he has repreſented it.—Let me look into theſe writings! Let me examine this account!—Handy!—[*Sitting.*] The book of fate could ſcarcely be more dreadful to me than this maſs of papers.

Enter Handy.

Handy. Sir!

Bev.

Bev. What do you do here, rafcal! I am bufy. How dare you interrupt me?

Handy. I thought you had called, Sir.

Bev. Get out of the room, firrah, or I'll——

Handy. I beg your pardon, Sir. I am gone, Sir. —What the deuce is the matter with him this morning? [*Exit.*

Beverley alone.

What an unfeeling animal is a mere perfon of bufinefs! Mr. Fable has ftunned me: I am thunder-ftruck: And yet there was a ferenity in his manner, a malicious calm in his countenance, that cut me to the foul—I am diftracted—I can. neither read, nor write, nor think.—Handy! Where are you, rafcal? [*Enter Handy.*] Why did not you take thefe things away, as I ordered you?

Handy. I thought you had not done breakfaft, Sir.—A card from Sir Charles Eafy, Sir. [*Giving it.*

Bev. Give me no cards, rafcal!

[*Throwing it away.*

Handy. The man waits for an anfwer, Sir.

Bev. I can fend no anfwer. I'm ill, I'm bufy, I'm——I'll fend an anfwer by-and-by—I'll fend an anfwer by-and-by.

Handy. Very well. I'll let him know, Sir. [*Exit.*

Beverley

Beverley alone.

Let me fee! let me collect my thoughts a little!
Suppofe I advife with Denier! fuppofe——

Enter Handy.

Handy. A letter, Sir!—requires no anfwer, they
fay.   [*Exit.*

Beverley alone.

From Lucy! I know her hand. [*Looking at the fu-
perfcription*] I muft look into it; but what poor
fpirits have I at prefent to perufe letters of gaiety!
Her tendernefs too—[*Opens and reads.*] What's this?

" Sir Harry Flutter has heard of your misfor-
" tunes, and convinced me that I fhould be a bur-
" then to you. He has offered to be my friend;
" fo adieu, Beverley!   Your's, Lucy."

Confufion!—the bufinefs is publick indeed then
—But fo foon to defert me!—To be the caft lover
of a caft miftrefs to half the town? But let her go!
let her go! an ungrateful jade! My friends will
execrate her. All my numerous acquaintance will
defpife her. She'll be the fcoff, the fcorn of——

*Enter Lord Riot, Sir Helter Skelter, Colonel Rakifh,
and Scanty.*

L. Riot. Beverley!—why, what the devil is all
this?

this? the whole town is talking of you. Is there any truth in this ftory? You are undone, they fay.

Bev. No; not undone, my lord.

Col. Rak. The St. James's Coffee-houfe is full of it; and Betty talks of nothing elfe.

Bev. Damnation!

Sir Helt. I was offered ten to one at the Cocoa-Tree, that you and all your partners would be in the Gazette next Saturday. Shall I take the odds, Beverley?

Bev. The houfe has not ftopt payment, Sir!—Confufion!

Scanty. No, no; not fo bad as that—a little crafh, indeed—but I faid the houfe would not ftop payment. I was always your friend, Mr. Beverley.

Bev. I am obliged to you, Sir.—Vexation!

Col. Rak. They fay, old Golding has made a fad hand of it in India. An old blockhead! What did he meddle for? Why, you could have ruined your-felf faft enough, without his affiftance—Poor little Lucy too! fhe'll be on the *pavée* again. I have half a mind to take compaffion on her myfelf.—But fhe's fo curfed fond of Beverley, there would be no dependance on her.

L. Riot. Well, but, Beverley! Your place at Wimbledon is to be put up at auction, it feems.—
A-going,

A-going, a-going, a-going!—So we are to have no dinner there next Sunday, I fuppofe?

Bev. No, no, no, no, my lord! Diftraction!

Sir Helt. As you'll part with that fet of bay ponies, and the phaeton, I fuppofe, I wifh you'd give me the refufal. You fhould think of your friends, Beverley.

Bev. Another time! another time, Sir!

L. Riot. Ay, I know we interrupt him. He is in the midft of all his writings and accounts, you fee. I fhall be glad to fee you, when you have leifure. Good day to you, Beverley!

Sir Helt. }
Col. Rak. } Adieu! adieu, Beverley!

[*Exeunt L. Riot, Sir Helt. and Col. Rakifh.*

Manent Scanty and Beverley.

Scanty. See what a fet of wafhy-minded fellows thefe are now!—It is well you are rid of them. Did not I always warn you to be cautious of your company?

Bev. I thank you for your advice; but it diftreffes me at prefent, Sir.

Scanty. Well, well, I'll fay no more then—I am glad to find matters not fo bad as they have been reported. You'll keep your head above water yet, I hope.—I juſt ſtaid to mention the affair of the twenty pounds you promiſed me, the laſt time I ſaw you.

Bev. This is not a time for affairs of that ſort, Sir.

Scanty. Well, well—I would not have mentioned it—but that laſt match at billiards was not quite ſettled, you know.

Bev. There, Sir—there's a bank-note of the value.—Now leave me, I beſeech you, Sir.

Scanty. Well, well,—I ſee you are buſy, and I will leave you—But for the future remember my counſel—ſtick to my advice—always be cautious in the choice of your company, Beverley! [*Exit.*

Beverley alone.

So, ſo, ſo, ſo!—This is *the world,* as they call it—A pack of hollow friends, and deſpicable ac-quaintance! How weak have I been, to give my heart to theſe wretches, who have ſouls incapable of mutual attachment! Callous to diſtreſs, and dead to the feelings of humanity!—How I long to ſee Denier! He is a true friend—frugal without ava-rice, and chearful without diſſipation. He would both advife and aſſiſt me.—He would pre-ſently——

Enter

Enter Denier.

Ha, Denier! I was this moment wiſhing for you. You have heard, I ſuppoſe!

Denier. I have, I have, Beverley; and ran to you immediately—though I had particular buſineſs in the city too this morning—but a friend has promiſed to tranſact it for me. How are you, Beverley?

Bev. What a blow, my friend! From whom had you the firſt news of it?

Denier. From Mr. Fable himſelf. He came to me on my own affairs, as well as about a large remittance which he has juſt received on account of Lydia.

Bev. Lydia!—Oh, Denier!—Lydia! [*Sighing.*] —a large remittance, did you ſay?

Denier. Yes, from her friends in India, who conſigned her to our family. A very conſiderable remittance, indeed! But Mr. Fable is made truſtee, I find. They treat her as the court of Chancery does a lunatick. We are committees of her perſon, and Mr. Fable committee of the eſtate.

Bev. Excuſe me, Denier! but the very ſhadow of mirth is at preſent unſeaſonable. I am glad, however, that Lydia is likely to be ſo amply provided for. [*Sighing.*

L 2 *Denier.*

Denier. So am I: and I am glad too that you have always profeſſed ſo total an indifference about her; as a diſappointment from any reverſe of fortune, in caſe you had fixed your affections on her, would have been an additional mortification.——But, Beverley!

Bev. My friend!

*Denier.*You are convinced, I believe, of the truth of my regard for you.

Bev. I never doubted it.

Denier. That I have the moſt affectionate friend-ſhip for you.

Bev. I am ſure of it.

Denier. You don't imagine me capable of pro-poſing any thing that might be diſagreeable to you?

Bev. The laſt man on earth I ſhould ſuſpect of it.

Denier. I think too, on your part, Beverley, that you would not, from a mere point of delicacy, op-poſe or repine at my happineſs, if it did not inter-fere with your own.

Bev. No, to be ſure, I ſhould not. But what is all this? Explain.

Denier. You muſt know then, Beverley, that I began very early to be captivated with Lydia.

Bev. Eh!

Denier.

Denier. But fancying you entertained a partiality for her, I fmothered my inclination out of friend-fhip for you. But as you meant only fuperficial gallantry, I now wifh to make her ferious pro-pofals.

Bev. Propofals to Lydia ?

Denier. Yes, propofals of marriage ; and indeed it feems almoft to have been the wifh of her friends to bring about fuch an alliance, by placing her in our family.

Bev. That's true—that did not occur to me at firft, I confefs—fhe too, I fuppofe, has given you fome hopes—I wifh you happy—I wifh you—I wifh you a great deal of happinefs, Mr. Denier.

[*Difordered.*

Denier. Thank you, my dear friend, thank you ! —But come, come, Beverley ! Mr. Fable's news has quite difheartened you. We muft not fee you too much caft down, neither. This is but a cloud. You will break out again with double fplendor prefently.—Can I be of any fervice to you ? Shall I look into your papers—and examine your accounts?

Bev. Not at prefent, I am obliged to you—not at prefent, Mr. Denier.

Denier. Oh, I had forgot. All my money is locked up : But if you fhould want a purchafer for

L 3   the

the Beverley eſtate, on that occaſion, I dare ſay, my friends would ſupply me. You may always command me, you know.

Bev. I know it. I am obliged to you.

Denier. Let me ſee! [*Looking at his watch.*] It is not ſo late as I thought it was—that Solomon is a puzzling, ſtupid, old fellow—I had better go up to the Alley, and look after the buſineſs myſelf, I believe—unleſs I could be of any uſe to you by ſtaying here, Beverley.

Bev. Not in the leaſt. I beg I mayn't hinder you.

Denier. Good day to you then! I can turn an eighth, I dare ſay, this morning. Good day, Beverley! [*Exit.*

Beverley alone.

Now am I completely miſerable. Fool, ideot, that I have been! to trifle with a delicate female heart—to trifle with my own!—Oh, Lydia! I am now, for the firſt time, thoroughly ſenſible of my affection for you;—and now to diſcover it, only to add to my wretchedneſs! Diſtraction!—Denier too ſeems to wear a different aſpect—at leaſt my imagination, jaundiced by my misfortunes, paints him of another colour.—But Lydia! after the im-pertinence of my former behaviour, how deſpicable muſt I appear to her! What a humiliating diſtance

has

has fortune now thrown between us!—Mrs. Golding here? New torture! Ha! Lydia with her! Oh, my heart! how fhall I look up to her!

Enter Mrs. Golding (in a morning difhabille.)

Mrs. Gold. Nay, come in, child! pray come in! I muft fpeak to poor Beverley. Come in, Mifs Lydia, I beg of you [*Beverley runs to the door and introduces Lydia*]—Ay, take care of her, kinfman! She is a delicate foul, and as much fhocked as if fhe were your fifter.—But, for Heaven's fake, child, what is this rigmarole ftory that Mr. Fable has diftracted us about?

Bev. A very ferious affair, indeed, madam.

Mrs. Gold. Serious! he's always ferious, I think —preaching, preaching, for ever preaching! Like lady Tott'nam, that builds all the Methodift chapels. —But it's a ftrange thing Mr. Golding fhould never write me word of all this bufinefs.

Bev. I have not yet examined the proofs; but dare fay, Mr. Fable has juft grounds for his proceedings.

Mrs. Gold. Lord, lord! how this breaks into all my arrangements! The glafs over my dreffing-room chimney-piece is ftuck round with cards, one upon another—I am promifed the whole town over

for

for thefe three months. But it's no matter—
they'll be the death of me—fo it don't fignify.

           [*Throws herfelf into a chair,*

Bev. We muft look forward, madam. The
profpect is a little gloomy at prefent, but promifes
to clear again. No endeavours fhall be wanting
on my part.

Mrs. Gold. No, I dare fay. You were always
a good creature—a great favourite of mine, you
know, always—But I can't tell what poffeffed them
to make you a Man of Bufinefs. If they had been
ruled by me, they would have put you into the
guards. You would have made a fweet figure in
a regimental: Would not he, Lydia? And then
you'd have had as little to do as Colonet Parade or
Captain Gilliflower. But I'll look into the red
book—the only book worth looking into—and fee
if we can't ufe our intereft to get you fome little
fnug finecure—a commiffioner of trade, perhaps,
or a lord of the admiralty.

Bev. I begin to feel we have no dependence but
on ourfelves, madam.

Mrs. Gold. Well, well—may-be not, kinfman
—and yet we have a very genteel fet of acquaintance.—But, mercy on me, what a figure do I
make, if any body fhould call, in this muflin
                                 fhade,

fhade, and queen's night-cap! Lydia, my dear! let me leave you here a minute or two, while I fhuffle on my things—and then come to me in my drefling-room. Your converfation is better than hartfhorn or lavender. .Poor Beverley here looks as difmal, as young lady Grizzle on her marriage with old Sir Solomon.   [*Exit.*

Manent Beverley and Lydia.

[*They remain fome time filent.*]

Bev. Excufe me, madam, if I venture to exprefs how deeply I am fenfible of your appearing to be affected by my misfortunes: And yet I cannot but confefs that I feel your compaffion almoft as painfully as a reproach—for I am confcious I have not deferved it.

Lydia. Touched as I am with the reverfe of your fituation, Mr. Beverley, I will not diffemble to you that I am pleafed with the change in your behaviour.

Bev. Still, ftill, this very approbation ferves to reproach me with the impropriety of my late conduct towards you. I feel it; I requeft your forgivenefs of it; and fhould be happy to pafs the reft of my life in endeavouring to atone it.

Lydia. Make no apologies to me, Mr. Beverley; I have

I have no right to expect them, nor has your conduct rendered them neceffary. Moft young gentlemen who pique themfelves on their knowledge of
the world, act much in the fame manner as you
behaved to me.

Bev. It is too true; but it is not the fwarm of
coxcombs that renders them lefs impertinent or
troublefome. I ought not to have adopted their
contemptuous airs, without being mafter alfo of
their tame infenfibility; yet I had youth to plead
in excufe for my vanities; and I flatter myfelf,
that time and reflection—and another motive, that
diftracts me when I think of it—might have rendered me an object lefs unworthy your compaffion.
Calamity has torn the veil from my eyes, and I
now fee, but too plainly, not only your excellence,
but my own imperfections.

Lydia. Calamity is a fevere mafter, yet amendment can fcarce be purchafed too dearly : And as
your errors have been venial, your diftrefs may be
but tranfient; nay, may, perhaps, at laft be the
means of your happinefs.

Bev. Impoffible ! impoffible ! However I may
be reftored to affluence, I can never, never tafte
of happinefs. I have thrown away—perhaps wan-
tonly too—I have thrown away the jewel that
fhould

should have been the pride and blessing of my life.
—Oh, Lydia! the feelings of worldly distress are
nothing to the agonies of a despairing affection.
My situation extorts from me what I have hitherto
endeavoured to conceal, even from myself. I love
you—I feel I long have loved you—though wretch
and fool enough to be almost ashamed of a passion
in which I ought to have gloried. I am now
punished for it—heaven knows, severely punished
—perhaps too severely—by losing the very hopes
of ever obtaining you.

Lydia. Do not run from one dangerous extreme
to another, Mr. Beverley; but guard against de-
spondency, as well as vanity and presumption. I
see you are much agitated, much dejected; and
what it would, perhaps, have been dangerous and
unpardonable to have owned to you but yesterday,
to-day I shall not scruple to declare. Hurried
away, as you were, by a torrent of fashionable vanities, and the poor ambition of keeping high
company, I thought I could discern in your mind
and disposition no mean understanding, nor ungenerous principles—too good for the associates
you had selected, and too susceptible not to be
in danger from such society. It is no wonder,
therefore, if I felt any growing partiality for you,
that I endeavoured to restrain it.

Bev.

Bev. To reftrain it! Say rather, to extinguiſh it.
—Oh, I now perceive all my wretchedneſs.—But,
to be ſupplanted by my boſom-friend! by Denier!

Lydia. I am at a loſs to comprehend you.

Bev. He confeſſed to me his paſſion for you
but this very morning—not an hour ago, he declared to me his intention of making you ſerious
propoſals.

Lydia. Such propoſals would be ſure of being
rejected—rejected with the utmoſt indignation.

Bev. What do I hear? May I ſtill hope then?
And are you reſolved not to liſten to his ad-
dreſſes? ·

Lydia. I am too well acquainted with his character. His manners, indeed, are lively, and his
worldly turn enables him to work himſelf into the
friendſhip of others; eſpecially, thoſe like yourſelf, Mr. Beverley—of an undeſigning open-heart-
ed character—in order to avail himſelf of their
foibles, promote his intereſt, and gratify his pe-
nury. Rely not too ſecurely on the warmth of
his profeſſions! Steady to no point but his intereſt,
you will find him ſhifting in his conduct, according
to the revolutions in your fortune. He ſeemed at
firſt deſirous to unite me to you; but now, hearing,
I ſuppoſe, of the alteration in your circumſtances,
and the late remittances in my favour, it is perfectly

fectly agreeable to his fentiments, to endeavour to fupplant you. As yet, however, he has made me no overtures.

Bev. So far then, at leaft, he is not unfaithful. But, oh, my Lydia! may I interpret your repugnance to his addreffes as an argument in my favour?

Lydia. I have already frankly declared my opinion of your character. It now remains with you to prove the truth of that opinion, and to determine my refolution accordingly. Do but bear up againft adverfity, fo as to fhew yourfelf equal to the poffible return of profperity—a trial, perhaps, ten times more dangerous—and be affured, Mr. Beverley, that, with the approbation of my friends, I fhall be happy to give every proof of my efteem for fo valuable a character.

Bev. My deareft Lydia! [*kiffing her hand*] Modeft, amiable Lydia! When you avow efteem, let me prefume to conftrue it affection! Oh, Lydia, you have made me fond of my misfortunes. Eafe and affluence corrupted me, and had fo weakened and enervated my mind, that the rough ftroke of adverfity would have ftunned me beyond the power of recovery, had not your gentle hand raifed me to the hope of happinefs. Take your

pupil,

pupil, Lydia; and render him—for you only can effect it—oh; render him worthy of fo dear, fo exquifite a monitrefs! [*Exeunt.*

A C T   III.

An Apartment in Golding's Houfe.

Enter Servant, fhewing in Tropick.

Servant.

WHAT muft I fay to Mr. Fable, Sir?

Trop. Only let him know that his old friend, Mr. Tropick, the fhip's hufband, defires to fpeak with him.

Serv. I fhall, Sir. [*Exit.*

Tropick alone.

Yes, I fhall fpeak to him—and pretty roundly too, I believe.—What times we live in! No morals, no order, no decency! Barefaced villainy at one end of the town, and villainy in a mafk at the other!—But my old friend here a hypocrite! I fhould almoft as foon have miftrufted myfelf. It is an unthankful office to give advice and reproof; but it is the duty, as well as privilege, of thofe who have been long acquainted with each other,

to

to let an old friend know, that all the world thinks him a fcoundrel.——Oh, here he is. I'll give it him—I'll lecture him—I'll——

Enter Fable.

Fable. Ha! my old friend, Tropick! How are you? how do you?

Trop. Well, very well.

Fable. I am glad on't; I rejoice to fee you.

Trop. May be fo, may be fo.

Fable. And your family?—All well, I hope.

Trop. All very well.

Fable. And the young fupercargo?—How does he go on?

Trop. Mighty well, mighty well.

Fable. Excellent!——And his elder brother, that was placed at Madrafs, is he removed to Bengal yet, as he propofed?

Trop. He is, he is; but——

Fable. That's right: Madrafs for health, Bengal for wealth!—that's the maxim there, you know.

Trop. Very true, very true; but——

Fable. And Mrs. Tropick too—How is fhe? How is your wife?

Trop. Pfhaw! let my wife alone! I want to fpeak with you, old Fable; I want to fpeak with you.

Fable.

Fable. Well; why don't you then?

Trop. Becaufe you hinder me. You ftop my mouth with enquiries, and won't let me fqueeze in a fyllable edgeways—A plague of your queftions!

Fable. Well, fpeak. I am all attention. What have you to fay to me?

Trop. Have you a friend or acquaintance in the world?

Fable. I think fo; fome few true friends, many more very fufpicious, and a number of common acquaintance.

Trop. And do you expect to keep one, that has common fenfe or common honefty, for the future?

Fable. Yes;—and yourfelf in particular.—But what's the matter? If you think I have done any thing wrong, it would be but friendly to tell me fo.

Trop. I came on purpofe to tell you; I came on purpofe to abufe you, old Fable.

Fable. I am obliged to you; but for what reafon?

Trop. Every honeft man fhould not only abhor a crime, but even keep clear of fufpicion.

Fable. Impoffible.

Trop. How fo?

Fable.

Fable. Both are not in his power. Not to be criminal, indeed, lies in his own breaft! but fufpicion and calumny, in the breafts and mouths of others. You confider yourfelf as an honeft man, I fuppofe.

Trop. Zounds! I know I am, without confidering at all.

Fable. And yet, honeft as you are, you could no more prevent my thinking you a rafcal, were I inclined to believe you one, than I could hinder your calling me fo.

Trop. I tell you, all the world calls you fo. It is the talk of the whole city—the Alley is full of it—the 'Change rings with it—and by and by, I fuppofe, the talkers in Leadenhall-ftreet will harangue about it. You are pretty well paragraphed already, old Fable.

Fable. I can't help their talking or writing. I can only take care not to deferve it.

Trop. Not deferve it!—Why, was not Golding, the great banker here, your old friend and acquaintance?

Fable. Moft intimately fo; moft confidentially; or, at his departure for India, he would fcarce have trufted his whole family and affairs to my care, with the particular charge of young Beverley.

VOL. II.   M   *Trop.*

Trop. Oh, did he fo ?—Now we are come to the point then.—And a fine guardian you have fhewn yourfelf—a pretty friend to Mr. Golding too! You have ftaggered the credit of the houfe, driven the poor young fellow almoft out of his fenfes, and made yourfelf his fole truftee and creditor. Every body fees what you drive at—but the court of Chancery may bring you to account yet, old Fable.

Fable. Let the parties file their bill at their plea-fure—or rather, do you be my chancellor.

Trop. I your chancellor !

Fable. Yes, you, my friend. I'll put in my anfwer immediately—but remember, that while I call upon your judgment in equity, I muft alfo infift on your fecrecy.

Trop. What ! keep it a fecret that you are an honeft man ?—Let all the world fuppofe you a fcoundrel ?

Fable. No matter. Don't let your zeal for my charaƈter teach them to unriddle the myftery at prefent ; but rather affift me in carrying on my projeƈt. Firft, however, promife filence. Give me your word, old friend.

Trop. My honour—Now you know you are fure of me.

Fable. I am convinced of it. You muft know, then,

then, that the danger of the houfe, and the ruin of young Beverley, is all a mere fiction.

Trop. A lie!—Zounds! to what purpofe?

Fable. The beft in the world.—A white lie, my friend! to refcue Beverley, and fave Mr. Golding.

Trop. A white lie?—I don't underftand you. Explain.

Fable. The young man was in the high road to deftruction, and driving at fuch a rate that he muft foon have overfet the whole undertaking.—It was time to pull the check-ftring.—To fpeak plainly; intoxicated as he was by pleafure and vanity, and countenanced by Mrs. Golding, who ought to have difcouraged him, direct advice would have been thrown away upon him. But could I ftand by a filent and inactive fpectator of the ruin of a whole family? No. Finding him incorrigible by fofter means, I conjured up the phantom of poverty. The meafures I have taken have already brought him to reafon; he promifes to become a new man; I fhall ultimately appear to be a true friend; and the credit of the houfe will be more firmly eftablifhed than ever.

Trop. I am fpeechlefs—ftruck dumb—you have taken my breath away—I have not a word to fay againft you—you are a very worthy, fenfible, honeft

fellow,

fellow, old Fable. You have redeemed your friend Golding, and will be the making of the young fellow's fortune.

Fable. Nay, I can't take the credit of his reformation entirely to myfelf neither. He is in love, it feems, with a moft amiable young lady, whofe tendernefs is redoubled by his misfortunes, while no calamity feems to affect his mind but the imaginary want of a fortune fuitable to his pretenfions to her.

Trop. And how can you anfwer it to yourfelf, to retain his money in your hands, when he wifhes to make fo laudable a ufe of it?

Fable. I don't mean to retain it. Finding Beverley in fo fair a way of amendment, I have already fet another wheel in motion, and (unknown to him) circulated a report of a fudden turn of fortune in his favour.

Trop. Unknown to him, d'ye fay?

Fable. Totally; and it is pleafant enough to fee how aukwardly he receives the civilities which are paid to him in confequence of this report, while, unconfcious of the caufe, he expects (according to the way of the world) nothing but flights and reproaches. To confirm the report, however, and to put him into good humour with himfelf again, I mean

I mean to fend a pretended agent or meſſenger to him, with letters and conſiderable remittances, as from Mr. Golding. All I want is a truſty perſon to diſcharge ſuch a commiſſion.

Trop. Can I be of any uſe to you?

Fable. Infinite, if you would undertake this negociation.

Trop. I!—Why, I am unknown in the family, 'tis true—but then the letters—Mr. Golding's hand, you know——

Fable. Oh, reaſons may be aſſigned for his making uſe of another hand.—Beſides, they won't be examined ſo nicely. You come to bring money, not to receive it—and that makes a wide difference. But we loſe time.—Will you aſſiſt me?

Trop. I will—hand and heart—body and ſoul, old Fable. Let me have the ſtores, ſails, maſts, and rigging, and I'll fit him out as handſomely as any veſſel I ever furniſhed in my life. You are a true-hearted, ſound-bottomed fellow, old Fable. But what an aſs have I made of myſelf!—Here did I come open-mouthed to reproach you for your roguery; and now you have perſuaded me to become your accomplice.

Fable. My ally—leagued in honour, not combined and confederated in villany. But, come with

M 3

me

me to my clofet, and I'll furnifh you with the needful.

Trop. I'll follow you; but I muſt, I muſt aſk your pardon firſt. It touched me to the quick to hear you were a rafcal, and I could not help telling you fo.—I beg your pardon again, and again, and again, my friend. You are one of the worthieſt men in the world—But, you know, there are not a more filly, empty, infolent, impudent, ignorant, lying vermin, than your framers of common reports, and collectors of perfonal paragraphs— wretches that pretend to know every thing, and know nothing. Your thoughts, words and actions, they know them all; what you have done; what you are doing, and what you intend to do, they know; know what a Papiſt tells his confeſſor, or the king whifpers the queen; things that never have been, will be, nor are like to be, ſtill they know—true or falfe, right or wrong, praife or blame, they don't care a halfpenny.—And I, to give a moment's credit to them! Forgive me this once, my friend; and for the future, without certain authority, I'll never believe a word I hear from common report, or depend upon a fyllable I read in the news-papers. [*Exeunt.*

Enter

The ſtreet.

Enter Lord Riot and Colonel Rakiſh.

Col. Rak. But do you think there is any truth in this report, my lord?

Lord Riot. Fact—you may depend upon't. A proctor from the city, who came to me about my ſuit with lady Riot, now depending in the Commons, told me that he heard it at the St. Paul's Coffee-houſe, from a gentleman that brought the news piping-hot from Sir George Sterling at Garraway's, and from other particular friends of old Fable.

Col. Rak. So then Beverley is upon his legs again, and Golding is not ruined, after all.

L. Riot. Full of treaſure as a mine, with a certain income as large as a jaghire—ſent home whole lacks of rupees by the laſt Indiaman, and buſhels of diamonds as plenty as Scotch pebbles.

Col. Rak. A lucky turn for Beverley! I wiſh I had known it before; I would not have black-balled him at Stapylton's; but, faith, I thought he had nothing for it but to ſhoot himſelf.

L. Riot. He is actually meditating a very deſperate action. I hear he is going to be married.

Col. Rak. Ay? to whom, my lord?

L. Riot.

L. Riot. Why, to mifs—Oh, here he is, to give an account of himfelf.

Enter Beverley.

How do you, how do you, Beverley? Nay, never look fo grave and ferious, man! I know you have no occafion. But why did you not call as I defired you, Beverley? I love to ferve you, and fhould have been very glad to fee you?

Bev. I am obliged to your lordfhip, but I have been engaged in particular bufinefs.

L. Riot. Bufinefs! You ufed to think pleafure your bufinefs.

Bev. And now, thank heaven, I have learnt to think bufinefs my pleafure.

Col. Rak. Ah, that's the true language of a man that is making a fortune and rolling in money, my lord. But, Beverley, my dear boy, why did you not call on me, if you ever thought there was the leaft fhadow of an occafion? You muft be fure that all I could command was entirely at your fervice.

Bev. I am obliged to you, colonel; but there was not the leaft neceffity for it.

L. Riot. No, no; fo it feems. I am very glad to hear it. Will you look in upon us at Almack's this evening, Beverley?

Bev.

Bev. It will not be in my power, my lord.

Col. Rak. We dine at the Tilt-Yard Coffee-houfe to-day. There is fome excellent claret. Will you go along with us, Beverley.

Bev. Not now, I thank you, colonel; I am going to Mr. Deniet.

L. Riot. Well; let us fee you foon; don't forfake your friends, Beverley.

Col. Rak. No; don't let us lofe you; come amongft us foon, my boy. In the mean time, I wifh you much joy.

L. Riot. So do I. Good day, Beverley!

Col. Rak. Good day, good day to you, Beverley!
[*Exeunt Lord Riot and Colonel Rakifh.*

Beverley alone.

Wifh me joy! what do they mean? furely, not to infult me! No, no; their manner was frank, and hearty, and cordial.—And yet, I thought they behaved oddly on the firft fhock of my affairs. But, perhaps, my fenfibility was too quick on that occafion, and my confufion on the breaking-out of my misfortunes made me fee every thing through a falfe medium. Yes, yes, I dare fay I wronged my friends, and I am heartily concerned at it.

Enter

Enter Cash.

Cash. Oh, Mr. Beverley, your fervant! I am glad I have found you. I have juſt been at your houſe to defire you to difcount theſe bills. They are indorſed by good men, and have not above a fortnight or three weeks to run, Sir.

Bev. Difcount, Mr. Cafh ? What do you mean ; You know I never venture to do any thing of that fort at prefent.

Cash. Not venture, indeed !—Well faid, Mr. Beverley ; you are pleafed to be pleafant.

Bev. I wifh you would pleafe to be ferious. I am ſo, I can affure you, Mr. Cafh.

Cash. What ! you won't difcount the bills then ?

Bev. No.

Cash. Confider the names at the back of them.

Bev. No matter. It don't fuit us.

Cash. " It don't fuit us,"—that's the banker's old anfwer in the negative.—When you're come to that, I am fure you won't do it—I am forry for it— I muſt try fome other houfe—Your fervant. [*Exit.*

Bev. Yours !—Now for Denier. [*Going.*

Enter Hazard.

Haz. Mr. Beverley ! one word with you, if you pleafe.

Bev.

Bev. [*turning.*] Mr. Hazard! Your pleafure, Sir?

Haz. We have a policy here on Sir Francis Racket, infured for a year for twelve thoufand—and we fhould be glad of your name at the bottom of it.

Bev. My name, Mr. Hazard!

Haz. If you pleafe, Sir.—There is a handfome premium, and Sir Francis is a very good life—He was fhewn at the coffee-houfe yefterday—a very good life—not above fix or feven and twenty—a little wild, indeed; but fuicide and the hands of juftice, you know, are always excepted.

Bev. I pretend to underwrite, Mr. Hazard! Do you want to ruin me entirely?

Haz. Ruin you! ha, ha, ha! ruin you—a very good jeft, faith—I wifh I was ruined your way, Mr. Beverley. [*Laughing.*

Bev. Do you laugh at me?

Haz. No, no—I don't laugh at you—but upon my word you make me merry, Mr. Beverley.—Poor ruined gentleman! ha, ha!—Will you fill up the policy, Sir?

Bev. No, not at fifty *per cent.* Sir. You know my fituation; and let me tell you, Sir, I look upon your application at this time as impertinent—particularly impertinent. [*Turns afide.*

Haz.

Haz. Know my fituation! Lord, how fome folks fwell on their good fortune! He is turning fine gentleman again already, I perceive.—Impertinent, quotha!—I wifh he would have fet his name to the policy, tho'—I would rather not have had an Ifraelite among the underwriters—however, let the worft come to the worft, we are fure of little Abraham at laft. Impertinent, indeed! [*Exit.*

Beverley alone.

This affront, among many other mortifications, is brought upon me by my paft folly and imprudence. Not only cenfured by the fenfible and the generous, but reproached by the bafe, ridiculed by the malicious, and infulted by the meaneft of mankind—Confufion!—But it is no wonder that I fhould be treated contemptuoufly by others, when my conduct has rendered me fo thoroughly defpicable even to myfelf. . [*Exit.*

An apartment in Denier's houfe.

Enter Lydia and Denier.

Lydia. Nay, ceafe, I befeech you, Sir! Do not, by urging me on a point fo very difagreeable, render it too painful a tafk to preferve that refpect for you, that I wifh to maintain!

Denier. Engaging Lydia! How much your
reserve

referve becomes you. Yet, let me flatter myfelf it is mere coynefs ; and thefe little pruderies; for fo I will fuppofe them—call forth new graces in your character, and revive the flame you would attempt to extinguifh.

Lydia. It is, however, with a peculiar ill grace, Sir, that you now pretend to difcover in me thefe latent qualifications.—You, who feemed lately fo defirous of recommending Mr. Beverley, and now, from what motive you know beft, honouring me with your own addreffes.

Denier. Beverley !—Beverley is convinced of my inviolable friendfhip for him—but it is no wonder, Lydia, that I, who had daily and hourly opportunities of contemplating your perfections, fhould be more deeply ftruck, than he that faw you but occafionally. I fhould not, however, fuch is my regard for him, have urged my own fuit, without being previoufly affured of his abfolute indifference.

Lydia. Indifference ! As to that, Sir, Mr. Beverley's indifference, or Mr. Beverley's partiality, in this inftance, is not at all material. I am placed in your family, it is true; and my fituation in life is not as yet pofitively afcertained. I was taught to believe, indeed, that I fhould ere now have been received and acknowledged by my friends:

But

But I confider fome late events as an earneft of their fpeedy appearance, and I truft they will offer no violence to my inclinations. I am determined, at leaft, in my own breaft ; and be affured, Sir, that no intereft, no force, no time, fhall fhake my refolution.

Denier. Your friends, madam, may poffibly be of a different opinion; and though I might not wifh them to put any conftraint on you, they will hardly be partial to the ruinous ftate of poor Beverley.

Lydia. In you, Sir, his intimate friend, fuch a reflection is particularly ungenerous: Yet do not prefume too much upon that notion, Sir! Whatever I may think of Mr. Beverley, fortune at leaft appears inclined to favour him.

Denier. Riddles! riddles, Lydia!

Lydia. You have not heard the late news then. He now feems as much courted by profperity, as he was but lately threatened by misfortunes: And I am this moment going with Mrs. Carlton, to give Mrs. Golding joy on the occafion.

Denier. And to congratulate Beverley?

Lydia. Perhaps fo—but be that as it may, you muft at leaft allow that I have dealt candidly with *you.* Grave as I may feem, Sir, I would not wifh to appear a prude ; and I fcorn all coquetry. [*Exit.*

Denier.

Denier alone.

Yes, yes; she's fond of Beverley, I fee—doatingly fond of him! and when a fentimental lady is once touched by a fond paffion, the rage is incurable.—But this fudden turn of fortune too in his favour—that I warrant has its effect with her—gold, gold, will have its weight—I shall foon know the particulars.—In the mean time, fuppofe I make a merit with Beverley of facrificing my paffion to him.—He certainly likes her; and it will be a cheap piece of generofity to refign that which I have no hopes of obtaining. I love to hufband my good offices: Ay, ay! that's the true policy! to gain the good will of others, without touching your own property.—Make a fmall prefent to thofe that you are fure want nothing at all, and it turns to account, like money put out at high intereft.—And ever, ever open your purfe, and offer to lend to thofe, who you know have no occafion to borrow!

Enter Beverley.

Ha! Beverley! you're welcome. Good day to you!

Bev. Good day, Denier! I was impatient to fee you.

Denier. Yes, I dare fay. I knew you would not

be

be long out of the house. But come; confess honestly, Beverley! Was this visit wholly designed
for me? Was it not partly—nay, chiefly—intended
for Lydia?

Bev. Lydia!—Lydia!—I should have been very
glad to see Lydia—I hope she is well.

Denier. Very well—and very much at your service—very much at your service, Beverley.

Bev. What do you mean?

Denier. I mean what I say—and I have been
thinking too on what passed at our last meeting,
Beverley.

Bev. On what subject?

Denier. Nay, nay; there is but one subject of
any consequence now, you know. But I am afraid
you dissembled with your friend a little. You
should be frank and generous with me. The commerce of friendship can't subsist without it; and I
have that title to the knowledge of what passes in
your breast, Beverley.

Bev. It was then in a state of insurrection, and
I was not master of its emotions, nor, indeed, well
able to marshal or distinguish them: But you know
I never scrupled to lay my heart open to you.

Denier. Why, to do you justice, I believe your
not being explicit, arose from the agitation of your

mind

mind at that inftant, rather than from want of fincerity—and I was a little flow of apprehenfion on
my part—but now we perfectly underftand each
other.—I fee you love Lydia: I am fure of it—
and, out of friendfhip and regard to you, my dear
Beverley—I frankly give up all my pretenfions to
her.

Bev. Generous, generous Denier!

Denier. Not at all—not at all—all my good offices
with her friends, my correfpondents in India, Mr.
Fable, and your own family, you have a right to
command.

Bev. Your kindnefs overwhelms me. How
fhamefully was I difpofed for a time to do injuftice
to friendfhip! I now defpife the mean and narrow
common-place maxims, of our friends falling off
from us. There is a jealoufy in the unfortunate—
an unworthy fufpicion of neglect and contempt
on account of their diftreffes—My flighteft acquaintance have given me proofs of their good
will, and your friendfhip is above all acknowledgment.

.*Denier.* I am happy in an occafion of teftifying
my unqueftionable regard for you.

Bev. I don't doubt it.

Denier. Depend on it.

Bev. My beſt friend!

Denier. My dear, dear Beverley!

[*Exeunt, preſſing hands, embracing, proteſting, &c.*

A C T IV.

An apartment in Golding's houſe.

Enter Fable and Check.

Fable.

THIS way, this way, Check! And are you ſure, quite ſure, this is faƈt?

Check. Too true, Sir.

Fable. Speculated in India-ſtock, do you ſay?

Check. To an incredible amount, Sir! here's the particular, Sir.

Fable. Let me ſee—let me ſee—[*looking at the paper.*] Confuſion!—and had you no knowledge or ſuſpicion of theſe tranſaƈtions till now, Check?

Check. Not the leaſt item, Sir. Little Smouſe the broker is but juſt gone, and ſays he has done more ſtock for my young maſter, than for half the reſt of the alley.

Fable. What imprudence! what madneſs!

Check.

Check. High play, indeed, Sir! Sir Charles Ducat of Mincing-lane, and my young master, it seems, have had the whole game between them. My young master is the bull, and Sir Charles is the bear. He agreed for stock, expecting it to be up at three hundred by this time; but, lack-a-day, Sir, it has been falling ever since.—You know the refcounter day, Sir; and if Mr. Beverley does not pay his differences within these four-and-twenty hours, the world cannot hinder his being a lame duck.

Fable. It scarce signifies what becomes of him—a prodigal!—But my friend Mr. Golding——

Check. Ay, if Mr. Beverley fails, the whole house must suffer, Sir. Having stood the late run upon us, our credit was firmer than ever.—But, after a tumble in the Alley, our notes will no more pass than a light guinea.

Fable. Is Mr. Beverley within?

Check. I thought I heard him come in just as I was following you hither, Sir.

Fable. Let him know I desire to speak with him.

Check. I will, Sir. [*Exit.*

Fable alone.

So!—To trifle with serious matters is playing with fire, I find. The ruin I counterfeited is now

becoming

becoming real; and the meafures I embraced to reform Beverley, and fave my friend, will only ferve to haften their deftruction. The fuddennefs of the alarm confounds me. The fhortnefs of the time too!—Oh, you are here, Sir.

Enter Beverley.

Bev. To attend your pleafure, Sir.

Fable. To witnefs your own irretrievable ruin, Sir!—How comes it, Mr. Beverley, how comes it, I fay, that you have hitherto kept your adventuring in the Alley, your infamous gambling in India-ftock, fo profound a fecret from me?

Bev. Spare your reproaches, Mr. Fable! They are needlefs. I know all my fault, and all my mifery. Ruin and infamy now ftare me in the face, and drive me to defpair. The vain hopes I had cherifhed of avoiding both are fruftrated; and there is not at this moment a more pitiable object than the wretch you now fee before you.

Fable. Pitiable! And what part of your conduct, Sir, has entitled you to compaffion?—To that compaffion, which the characteriftick humanity of this nation has ever fhewn to the unfortunate?—fometimes, indeed, to the imprudent?—Have you, Sir, any claim to this? You, who have fo grofly abufed the mutual confidence between

man

man and man, and betrayed the important truft repofed in you—What! a banker! a banker, Mr. Beverley, not only fquandering his own fortune, but playing with the property of others!—the property of unconfcious perfons filently melting away, as if by forgery, under his hands, without their own prodigality!—And is fuch a man, becaufe he is at length buried in the ruin he has pulled down on others, an object of compaffion? No, Sir, nothing is to be lamented but the mildnefs of his punifhment.

Bev. The very atrocioufnefs of his crime, the pungency of his guilt and remorfe, which put him upon a rack feverer than any penal laws could devife, ftill render him an object of pity.

Fable. Your remorfe and reformation, I fear, were but hypocrify. Where was that ingenuous confidence that would elfe have prompted you to lay open this dark tranfaction, as well as the reft of your unjuftifiable extravagance? Your candour, in that inftance, would at leaft have argued the fincerity of your profeffions, and afforded a real proof of your penitence.

Bev. Oh, Sir, do not attribute my filence to deceit! I had been taught to hope and believe that the event would have proved profperous; and

thought

thought to have furprifed you, and charmed Lydia, with my unexpected good fortune. But, oh,
what a cruel reverfe have I now to experience!

Fable. A reverfe that the daily experience of
thoufands might have warned you to avoid, rather
than to build your hopes on fuch a fandy founda-
tion. The tide of eaftern riches flowing in upon
us, which might have fcattered plenty over our
country, fuch adventurers as you, Mr. Beverley,
have rendered the parent of poverty, and the
means of almoft general bankruptcy. A fimple
individual to rife to-day worth half a million—an
undone man to-morrow! Are thefe the principles
of commerce? Were thefe the leffons which your
worthy father tranfmitted to you? or which I
have inculcated?

Bev. Have mercy, Mr. Fable; confider my
fituation, and do not feek to aggravate the horrors
of it! I who fo lately thought myfelf in the road
to profperity, hoping to retrieve my fortune, and
redeem my character, now fhortly to be branded
as the moft faithlefs of beings, the bafeft of mankind! Diftraction!

Fable. Your fituation, I own is dreadful; but by
what an unpardonable complication of depravity
have you brought it upon yourfelf, Mr. Beverley!
Not

Not content with one fpecies of enormity, but in-
duftrioufly multiplying your ruin, and combining
in yourfelf the double vices of a Man of Bufinefs,
and a Man of Pleafure! Gambling the whole morning in the Alley, and fitting down at night to
quinze and hazard at St. James's ; by turns,
making yourfelf a prey to the rooks and fharks
at one end of the town, and the bulls and bears at
the other ! Formerly, a young fpendthrift was
contented with one fpecies of prodigality—but it
was referved for you and your precious affociates
to compound this new medley of folly, this olio
of vice and extravagance, at once including the
diffolutenefs of an abandoned debauchee, the chi-
canery of a pettyfogger, and the dirty tricking of
a fraudulent ftock-jobbing broker.

Bev. Go on ; go on, Sir ! it is lefs than I merit,
and I can endure it with patience. My late hu-
miliation was but the prologue to my total ruin.
The moft defperate calamity cannot now make
me more miferable.

Fable. Oh, Beverley ! did you but know the con-
folation I had in ftore for you, the fchemes I had
formed to make you eafy in your circumftances,
and happy in your love, you would ftill more re-
gret this cruel difappointment.

Bev.

Bev. Happy in my love !—Oh, Lydia, I dare not even think of my prefumption in having afpired to your favour !

Fable. Go, young man ! go to thofe friends on whom you formerly placed fuch reliance, and try what they will contribute to deliver you from ruin !—Leave me a while—ftudying to exert my weak endeavours to preferve my friend—or, if they fail, ftruggling to arm my mind with fortitude and patience.

Bev. Where fhall I direct myfelf ? to whom fhall I apply ? My fituation, I fear, is hopelefs. The inhabitant of a dungeon, under fentence of execution, is in a ftate of happinefs, to what I feel at this moment.   [*Exit.*

Fable alone.

Tho' he appears at this inftant fo very culpable, I cannot but be touched by his agitation and re- morfe.—Yet this is not a moment for paffion, but reflection.—The ruin, if not prevented, fo tho- roughly overwhelming ! The time fo preffing ! My friend abfent ! The property I can command, large and confiderable as it is, not to be converted into fpecie directly !—What can be done ?—Mr. Tropick muft return me the money in his hands, which

which I muſt now prevent his delivering, as well
as the ſuppoſed letters to Beverley—yet that
will be far, very far from ſufficient—how to make
up the reſt then ?—There is one way indeed—but
is that warrantable ? Lydia's truſt-money.—Have I
a right, on any pretence whatever, to lay my hands
but for a moment, on that ſacred depoſit ?—And
yet, where would be the injury ? I am ſure of re-
placing the ſum before there is the leaſt probability
of its being demanded ; and that reſource, in
conjunction with others already in my power,
would ſupply every emergency. My abſent friend
would be reſcued from certain ruin, even the tranſ-
greſſion of Beverley might be concealed from the
world, and Lydia would ſuffer no wrong, nor even
be alarmed by ſuſpicion.—It ſhall be ſo. I'll ſee
this broker, and ſettle the matter immediately.—
And yet, my heart recoils at this tranſaction.
The moſt pious frauds are at leaſt ambiguous ;
and I feel it as the moſt cruel neceſſity to be
driven to indirect means, even for the moſt generous purpoſes.—But I have entangled myſelf by
one crooked action, and I muſt endeavour to redeem
all by another.   [*Exit.*

Another

Another apartment in the fame houfe.

Enter Handy and Mrs. Flounce.

Handy. Oh! if this be the cafe, I fhall give warning immediately.

Mrs. Flounce. So fhall I, I promife them. Ruined indeed! In my mind it is a monftrous piece of impudence in thefe trumpery merchant-people to keep gentlefolks for their fervants, like people of quality.—Mrs. Golding quotha!—a gentlewoman of my genteel family—as wealthy a rope-maker's daughter as any in the city of Briftol! equal to Mrs. Golding, I hope, at any time.

Handy. Equal, Mrs. Flounce! ay, and a great deal fuperior. An old worn-out bit of beggar's-tape, that binds the hem of quality!—imitating countefses and duchefses—endeavouring to adapt her vulgar weft-country airs to the meridian of St. James's—aping, in her Briftol manner, the airs and graces of perfons of fafhion—but no more like perfons of fafhion, than a Briftol ftone is to a diamond!

Mrs. Flounce. Well! fervice, as they fay, is no inheritance, Mr. Handy—fo I fha'n't go into place again—not I, truly—I have taken a houfe at Hogfden,

Hogſden, and intend to ſet up a boarding-ſchool to teach young ladies breeding.

Handy. And you'll have great ſucceſs, I dare ſay, Mrs. Flounce.—As to me, my maſter was to have got me a good place in the India-houſe; or to have ſent me out with the next cargo of judges and generals to Bengal.—But now he's ruined in the Alley, his intereſt I ſuppoſe is all gone— as well as his principal—eh, Mrs. Flounce? But this is always the caſe, when Lombard-Street will travel to Pall-Mall. Quite another latitude! Is not it, Mrs. Flounce?—But odſo! here's ſome-body coming up ſtairs—we'll ſettle this matter in the houſekeeper's room. Your hand, my dear!

Mrs. Flounce. And my heart too, Mr. Handy! but I ſhall pick a quarrel with my lady, and give warning as ſoon as ſhe comes home.

Handy. To be ſure, Mrs. Flounce! There's nothing more to be got in this houſe. We'll both give warning immediately; and we'll give up the month's wages to the poor devils, out of mere charity. [*Exit.*

Enter a Servant, followed by Golding.

Gold. Mr. Fable not at home, d'ye ſay?

Serv. But juſt gone out, Sir.

Gold.

Gold. Nor Mr. Beverley?

Serv. No, Sir.

Gold. Nor Mrs. Golding neither?

Serv. My lady has been abroad with two other ladies moſt part of the morning, but we expeƈt her home very ſoon, Sir.

Gold. Well—well—as ſoon as any of them return, let me know.

Serv. I will, Sir.   [*Exit.*

Golding alone.

Very ſtrange all this! I don't underſtand one word I have heard or read of my friends, or myſelf, or my affairs, ſince I landed. Thou art in a maze, friend Golding! But a man who comes home from the Indies, muſt expeƈt at his return to meet with ſome new events to ſurpriſe him—his houſe burnt, his daughter eloped, his ſon engaged in a fray, his wife dead, or ſome little accident. The principal objeƈt of my voyage too has not yet anſwered, though in other points it has amply ſucceeded. I long to ſee Mr. Fable, or Beverley, or my wife—Who have we here?

Enter Tropick.

What is your pleaſure, Sir?

            Trop.

Trop. To fpeak with Mr. Beverley. But he is not at home, they fay.

Gold. So it feems, Sir.

Trop. Having fome very particular bufinefs with him, I muft beg leave to wait for his return.

Gold. I am concerned in Mr. Beverley's affairs. Pray, Sir, what is your bufinefs? You may truft it to me, Sir.

Trop. I have letters of great confequence from abroad to deliver to him, and fome more to Mr. Fable.

Gold. From abroad! From what part of the world? and from whom, Sir?

Trop. From India—from my old friend and acquaintance, Mr. Golding.

Gold. Mr. Golding!—So, here's an old friend and acquaintance of mine that I never faw in my life before. [*afide.*]—And pray, how is Mr. Golding, Sir?

Trop. Never better, Sir.

Gold. Where is he at prefent, Sir?

Trop. In India, Sir.

Gold. What part of India?

Trop. Bengal.

Gold. I don't know that ever I had the pleafure of feeing Mr. Golding. Pray, what fort of a man is he?

Trop.

Trop. As good a fort of man as breathes, Sir.

Gold. Yes; but his perfon?

Trop. Oh, as to his perfon, that is indifferent enough—a little, wizen, withered, whipper-fnapper old gentleman, fhorter by the head and fhoulders than you or I, Sir.—A little merry man though —many a curry have I eat in his company— many a fagar have little Goldy and I fmoaked together.

Gold. What! you and little Goldy are particular friends then?

Trop. Very particular; or he hardly would have entrufted me with my prefent commiffion, I believe.

Gold. What may that commiffion be, Sir?

Trop. Nay, I may tell you: and indeed the affair will foon be known by every body.—I am not only commiffioned to deliver the letters I mentioned, but charged with a very capital remittance from my friend Golding, configned to Mr. Fable, in favour of the young gentleman here, Mr. Beverley, for whom I now came to enquire.

Gold. And have you this capital remittance with you at prefent, Sir?

Trop. Yes, yes; I have my credentials. Here they are! [*clapping his hand to his pocket*] fafe

and

and found, I warrant you—and as good as the Bank, Sir.

Gold. And you had this money directly from Mr. Golding, you fay?

Trop. From his own hands—from whom elfe fhould I have it?

Gold. Nay, how fhould I know? But it is very well as it is—very well. Be fo good then, if you pleafe, Sir, to deliver this very capital fum of money to me, Sir!

Trop. To you? On what account, friend?

Gold. Becaufe, as you fay, you had it from me.

Trop. Why, who are you?

Gold. The very perfon from whofe own hands, you confefs, you received it—Mr. Golding.

Trop. You Mr. Golding!

Gold. The fame.

Trop. No, no—not you indeed—that will never pafs, I promife you.

Gold. Not Mr. Golding!—Why, who the devil am I then?

Trop. A damn'd rogue, I believe. Juft now you faid, you did not know Mr. Golding; and as foon as you heard I had brought a confiderable fum of money you are turned into Mr. Golding yourfelf.—But you may caft your fkin again, old ferpent. The trick won't take, I affure you.

Gold.

Gold. Trick!—This is the moſt impudent piece of knavery!—Trick, indeed! I believe, there is ſome trick upon me here, if I knew what to make of it—I'll have you taken up for a new kind of forgery; for bringing money upon falſe pretences —for——

Trop. And you inſiſt upon it, that you are Mr. Golding?

Gold. To be ſure, I do. I'll call the whole houſe to prove the truth of it.

Trop. And Mr. Golding, the true Mr. Golding, is really returned from India then?

Gold. To be ſure he is. Can't you ſee, Sir?

Trop. I have made a fool of myſelf a ſecond time—that's what I ſee—but be who you will, Mr. Golding, or not Mr. Golding, I ſhall not deliver the letters or money to you, old gentleman!—I'll go back again, like a fool as I came—to the old fool that ſent me—on ſuch a fool's errand!

[*Exit.*

Golding alone.

What the plague, am I in India ſtill then? or in the moon? and myſelf and the people about me all lunaticks?—Our affairs they ſay are all in con-fuſion, and yet Beverley is going to be married.— To whom, I wonder!—No matter who—the match I intended will be quite out of the queſtion——

Another

Another piece of ill fortune!—But I am in the dark all this while—talking of every thing, and acquainted with nothing.—Well! since I can find nobody, and get no intelligence at home, I will seek for it abroad—by delivering my letters, and making enquiries at Mr. Denier's [*going.*]—But stay! here's a woman at last. My wife, I hope.—Hey! how's this? Do I see right? Mrs. Carlton!

Enter Mrs. Carlton.

Of all the women on earth, Mrs. Carlton!

Mrs. Carlt. Mercy on me! what do I see? Can that be Mr. Winterton?

Gold. No.

Mrs. Carlt. Yes; it is he.

Gold. No, no, no, I tell you!

Mrs. Carlt. What! sha'n't I believe my senses? Are not you Mr. Winterton?

Gold. Hush!—I am glad to see you—You know me well enough—but don't call me by that name again for the life of you!

Mrs. Carlt. Why, your name is Winterton—isn't it, Sir?

Gold. Hist! don't bawl so—Come away from that door a little—and not a breath of that name, I charge you.

Mrs. Carlt. Lord, Lord! what's the matter with you?—What's the man fo much afraid of?

Gold. What moft men are afraid of—my wife.

Mrs. Carlt. Your wife!

Gold. Ay! Mrs. Golding. Now you are fatisfied.

Mrs. Carlt. What, and are you Mr. Golding then, after all, Sir?

Gold. I believe fo. I was Mr. Golding before I went abroad—but I fcarce know who I am, or what I am, or where I am, fince I came back again.

Mrs. Carlt. So this was the reafon then that we, poor fouls, could never difcover what was become of you, Mr. Winterton—Mr. Golding, I beg your pardon, Sir. But you need not be fo terrified—for I left Mrs. Golding on a morning vifit, and fhe is not come in yet.

Gold. In the mean while, let us make the beft ufe of our time then. Where is my daughter? where is Lydia?

Mrs. Carlt. I left her with Mrs. Golding. You'll fee them both here prefently.

Gold. That's well—but we muft be cautious—How does fhe do?

Mrs. Carlt. As well as can be expected in her fituation.

Gold.

Gold. As well as can be expected!—What do you mean?—Her fituation!—Not undone, I hope.

Mrs. Carlt. Only over head and ears in love, Sir.

Gold. In love! with whom?

Mrs. Carlt. With the young gentleman of this houfe—Mr. Beverley.

Gold. Beverley!—Why, he is going to be married.

Mrs. Carlt. So they fay, Sir.

Gold. But to whom? do you know?

Mrs. Carlt. To her, Sir.

Gold. To Lydia?

Mrs. Carlt. Yes, to be fure, Sir. Heaven forbid it fhould have been any body elfe!—But his affairs are all in confufion, it feems, and there's fuch a pother between them, that I am half diftracted about it.

Gold. And I am quite diftracted—diftracted with joy, Mrs. Carlton! Heaven be praifed!—Come, come! here is one piece of good fortune, however!—Leave young folks to themfelves, I fay.—What I have been labouring and ftudying to bring about, have they fettled at once. The very thing I could have wifhed! Half the purpofe of my voyage to India, and the meaning of the money lately remitted, for which Mr. Fable is appointed truftee.

Mrs.

Mrs. Carlt. And does Mr. Fable know any thing of her relation to you, Sir?

Gold. Not a fyllable—Heaven be praifed, not a fyllable!—I was not willing to explain the matter, till I faw more likelihood of my fcheme's taking place.—And now from what I can judge of his proceedings, it is lucky that I never trufted him. An old fox! a caterpillar! a viper! Beverley's fole truftee and creditor indeed!—a crocodile!

Mrs. Carlt. But was it not a little cruel in you to keep us fo long in the dark, Mr. Golding?

Gold. Nay, I have not been fo much to blame neither, Mrs. Carlton. My firft marriage, with Lydia's mother, when I was an idle young fellow, was a foolifh love bufinefs—and I knew that my having a daughter abroad would have been an ob-jection to my prefent wife's relations—fo I fairly kept the whole matter a fecret.—Lydia's mother dying in child-birth, and my prefent marriage having taken place during the infancy of Lydia, I directed her to be educated by another name, under which I once vifited you and my daughter in India —that's the whole affair!—But not a word more of the name or the bufinefs, I charge you!

Mrs. Carlt. Not for the world, Sir, till you think proper to mention it.

Mrs.

Mrs. Gold. [*behind.*] Defire mifs Lydia to fee the things taken out of the coach, and then to follow me into the drawing-room!

Mrs. Carlt. Ha! the ladies are here—here already, I proteft, Sir.

Gold. Yes, I hear my wife's voice. I would not have her furprize us together. I might appear fomewhat aukward and confufed, perhaps. I'll run and give her the meeting—but remember now, not a wry word for your life! Mum, mum, Mrs. Carlton! [*Exit.*

Mrs. Carlton alone.

You may depend upon me, Sir.—Ah, Mr. Golding, Mr. Golding! there is no trufting to looks, I find. Who would have thought of your paffing by a wrong name? Who would have fufpected fuch a grave, demure-looking gentleman?

Enter Mr. and Mrs. Golding.

Mrs. Gold. My dear love! I am tranfported to fee you. This is the moft agreeable furprize—I thought the laft fhips that came in would have brought me nothing but letters—or, perhaps, a pagoda, or a monkey at beft. But, my hufband! —my dear love!—Oh, my dear, let me introduce a very agreeable, genteel young lady to you!—

O 3   a young

a young lady of fortune and family, I aſlure you.
—My huſband, my dear child! [*Introducing Lydia.*]
My dear, miſs Lydia Winterton!

Lydia. Ha! my father! Mr. Winterton!

[*Faints away.*

Mrs. Gold. She faints away! Take care of the
child!

Maids enter, and run to aſſiſt Lydia.

Lord! what's the meaning of this?—She cried
out, *father!* and called you Mr. Winterton.

Gold. Yes—ſhe did ſay ſomething about Bet-
terton.

Mrs. Carlt. Ay, the poor child has very weak
ſpirits—Every little thing flutters her.—And Mr.
Golding is a little like her papa too, I think—
eſpecially about the noſe.

Gold. Ay; may be ſo—may be ſo—but, my
dear, ſuppoſe you take her into your chamber, and
let her lie down a little to recover her ſpirits!

Mrs. Gold. Ay; we'll ſoon bring her to herſelf
again—This way, Molly—keep the eau de luce to
her noſe.—This is from riding backwards in the
coach, I fancy—This way; gently, Molly! gently.

[*Mrs. Gold. and maids lead out Lydia.*

Manent

Manent Mrs. Carlton and Golding.

Gold. So, fo! here was an efcape! Murder will out.

Mrs. Carlt. Never fear, never fear, Sir! I'll go in to Lydia directly—let nobody be about her but myfelf—and as foon as fhe recovers, I'll teach her her leffon, and give her the right cue, I warrant you.

Gold. Ay, do fo, do fo, Mrs. Carlton! Take care, I befeech you! For the fake of peace and quietnefs, keep this matter a fecret! I fhall never be able to break it to Mrs. Golding—fhe would think herfelf injured, cheated, robbed, and undone. —And if fhe were once to know Lydia was a daughter of mine, fhe would ring it in my ears as long as I live—a fmoaky houfe, and a fcolding wife, you know! I need fay no more—It is a kind of hell to inhabit one, and the devil himfelf would fcarce live with the other. [*Exeunt.*

ACT

A C T V.

An apartment in Denier's houſe.

Denier and Capias.

Denier.

VERY well, very well!—And you have him ſafe then, Mr. Capias?

Capias. Safe and ſecure, I warrant you, Sir. I put the writ into ſure hands—thoſe that will touch a man, let him be ever ſo ſhy. However, they had not much ado in this inſtance—They planted themſelves at the corner, ſtopt Mr. Golding near his own door, and told him their buſineſs: He went with them at once, and is now lodged with my friend Snap in Shire-Lane.

Denier. This comes from early intelligence. No miniſter, no general, no broker, could turn it to greater advantage.

Capias. But how did you procure it, Sir? You are the firſt upon the roll—I ſearched the ſheriff's office, and there is nothing elſe out againſt Mr. Golding, or any body connected with him.

Denier.

Denier. Beverley, knowing me to be his friend, came to acquaint me with his diftrefs in the Alley. The natural confequences of that adventure are obvious: And all my India concerns, remittances, and money tranfactions coming through their houfe, it ftruck me with a panick; but, by good luck, he was fcarce gone before I had notice of Mr. Golding's return by letters from India, brought by the fame fhip in which he came over. I did not lofe a moment. I dare fay he had not once entered his doors when the officers met him, and perhaps Beverley himfelf is not yet apprifed of his arrival. Am not I a man of difpatch, Mr. Capias?

Capias. A Cæfar, a Machiavel, Sir! You know all the turnings and windings and narrow back-ftairs of the law too. You feel your own way; and are client, counfel, and attorney, all in one, Sir!

Denier. And have you the deed ready, Capias?

Capias. Here it is, Sir, perufed, figned, and fettled, by old Steady, of Lincoln's Inn—an excellent workman! and if we can prevail on Mr. Golding to execute it, you'll come in for an exclufive lien upon his effects, inftead of compounding with the other creditors under a commiffion of bankruptcy, which I fuppofe will be taken out in lefs than thefe three days.

Denier.

Denier. Ay—and under which they will not pay five fhillings in the pound, perhaps—fuch a tumble!—fign the deed? tell him he muft fign it—His mind's unfettled yet, and he'll be eafily perfuaded—Befides, he'll be glad to ferve a particular friend—It can't affect him, you know—the affignees will divide the remainder.—I have been a conftant friend to the houfe—he'll be glad to return the obligation, and I fhall fall upon my legs again.

Capias. Let us lofe no time; the fooner he executes the better, Sir!

Denier. Come along then! I'll attend you to Mr. Snap's. I have not feen Mr. Golding fince his return, and we fhould vifit our friends in their affliction, you know. Come along, Mr. Capias!

[*Exeunt.*

Scene changes to a room in Snap's houfe.

Fable and Snap.

Fable. Every thing much to my fatisfaction; nothing here to complain of, I affure you, Mr. Snap. I never was more comfortably lodged in my life, never wifh for better attendance, or more convenient accommodation.

Snap. We does all in our power to oblige company,

pany,

pany, Sir.—Nobody can do no more, you know—
efpecially fuch as behaves like gentlemen, like your
honour, Sir—for we has them of all forts.—
Within this fortnight, there has been no lefs than
four or five different lodgers in this very apartment.—The room is genteel enough for that matter.—Let me fee, who was they?—An enfign in
the guards; a poet-man from Paddington; a
Scotch actor-man! an old battered lady from
Soho; and a very fine young one from the New
Buildings at Marybone—that's five—and now we
have the honour of your honour to make up the
even half-dozen, Sir.

Fable. I hope not to give you much trouble,
Mr. Snap.

Snap.) No, no; you knows you'll foon be reliev-
ed, I dare fay, your honour.

Fable. Were my letters all delivered according to
the directions?

Snap. Every one, Sir; and the gentlefolks fays
they will be here prefently.—I thinks I hears fomebody at the door now.—Shall I fhew them up, Sir?

Fable. If you pleafe, Mr. Snap.

Snap. Perhaps, they chufes fome refrefhment.—
I've fome fine dry fherry—very good for a whet in
the morning.

Enter

Enter Tropick.

Fable. Ha! my friend, I am happy to fee you.—
Mr. Snap, good morning to you.

Snap. Gentlemen, your fervant.—Shall I fend up
a bottle of white wine, or a bowl of punch, Sir?

Fable. Not at prefent, I thank you, Mr. Snap.—
If any body elfe enquires for Mr. Golding, be fo
good as to fhew them up.

Snap. I will, Sir.—Your fervant—Gentlemen,
your fervant.   [*Exit.*

Manent Fable and Tropick.

Fable. This is kind, my friend. You little thought
of my defiring a vifit from you at this houfe, I
believe.

Trop. Look ye, Fable, I don't know what to
make of all this.—I don't underftand you.—You
may be an honeft man, perhaps.—I hope you are
an honeft man; but you look very much like a
rogue at prefent, I can tell you.—Firft of all, you
employ me in a damned ridiculous bufinefs, in
which I have made a curfed fool of myfelf—and
that is fcarce over, than in comes a note from you
at a fponging-houfe, defiring me to come there,
but not to afk for you by your own name. What's
the meaning of all this, mafter Fable?

                                         Fable.

Fable. No harm, I affure you, friend. In regard to the bufinefs you mention, I meant to ftop your going, if, unluckily, it had not been too late; and as to your not afking for me here by my own name, I defired it, becaufe I am not here in my own right, but as the reprefentative of another perfon.

Trop. Another perfon! I underftand you lefs and lefs. Why, zouns, man, they can't arreft people by proxy.

Fable. No; but they may by miftake; and I have humoured the miftake, in order to ferve the real party, and punifh the rafcally creditor.

Trop. Who is the real party? and who is the creditor?

Fable. The writ was fued out againft Mr. Golding, at the fuit of Mr. Denier. I had but juft fettled fome affairs very effential to Mr. Golding's intereft; and did not know of his return till the moment I had placed him beyond danger. Coming home, however, in the dufk of the evening, the catchpoles lay in wait near the houfe, touched me on the fhoulder, and prefented their authority. I readily obeyed; fubmitting to an arreft in the character of Mr. Golding, and glad of an opportunity of expofing the falfe profeffions of a pretended friend to the family.

Trop.

Trop. Well, this feems right enough;—and yet, fome how, I don't like it neither.—I don't love turning and doubling.—I love to go ftraight forwards, Mr. Fable.

Fable. The beft road will wind fometimes, you know. Have a little patience; we fhall foon be at the end of our journey.

Enter Snap.

Snap. More company, Sir.—Walk up, gentlemen; walk up, ladies. The ftairs is a little dark; but there's no danger.

Enter Golding, Mrs. Golding, Mrs. Carlton, Lydia,
and Beverley.   [*Exit Snap.*

Fable. Mr. Golding, I am happy to fee you returned.—Ladies, you're welcome.—Beverley, how do you?—Well, Mr. Golding, how do you like my new apartments?

Gold. Like?—I like nothing I have feen or heard of you fince my coming from the Indies. Out of doors, I hear you have almoft made me a bankrupt; at home, I find you have made me a fool.

Fable. How fo, Mr. Golding?

Gold. Have not you made yourfelf this young gentleman's fole truftee and creditor?

Fable.

Fable. He has made me so, I confess.

Gold. And did not you persuade him to it by a Canterbury tale of letters from me, losses in India, and the devil knows what,—when you had no more authority to talk of me, than of the pope or the great mogul ? Had you any such letters from me? Answer me that, Sir.

Fable. No, I had not.

Gold. I told you so.—And did you ever hear that I had any losses in India?

Fable. Never.

Gold. There again !—Did not I tell you so?— And what the plague did you mean by all those falshoods and forgeries ? Eh, Mr. Fable ?

Fable. To serve you, and maintain the credit of the house.

Gold. And a very creditable way our affairs are in, truly! One moment I learn that you are our sole creditor ; and the next moment I find that our sole creditor is so much in debt himself, that he is lodged in a sponging-house.

Fable. Very true ; even so, Sir.

Trop. Psha ! plague of your cool blood ! I can't bear it. Why does not the man speak out, and tell the whole story ?—Look ye, Mr. Golding ; he is a very honest fellow ; and all he has done was entirely for your service.

Gold.

Gold. Oh ho, Sir! Are you there, old Smoke-a-pipe? What, my old friend, that eat curries and smoked fagars with me at Bengal!—are you come again?—Where's the money I sent by you?

Trop. There, old Fable; you see what a pretty figure I have made.

Fable. Mr. Golding will soon know you better, and entertain a proper refpect for you.

Gold. I am finely entertained by you both. You speak for him, and he vouches for you—and I don't know what to make of either of you. But, to come to a right understanding, be so good as to tell me, Mr. Fable, whether you did not receive a very large remittance from India, in favour of this young lady?

Fable. I did.

Gold. Very well.—You muft know then, Sir, that her friends have appointed me joint-truftee, with a power to pay the whole fum into her own hands immediately. She has a prefent occafion for it, and defires to receive it directly.

Lydia. I do, I do, Sir, in order to apply it for the relief of Mr. Beverley.

Bev. Generous, too generous Lydia! Ruin fhould not prevail on me to touch a fingle doit of it.

Gold.

Gold. Pleafe to let us touch it, however, Mr. Fable.

Fable. Impoffible.

Gold. Impoffible! how fo? You received it fafe—did not you?

Fable. I do not deny it.

Gold. Where is it then?

Fable. Not in my hands at prefent; nor can I advance any part of it within this fortnight or three weeks.

Gold. Three weeks!—We can't ftay three days, or three hours, Sir.

Bev. My Lydia defrauded too!—Confufion!

Mrs. Carlt. The child's money gone!

Trop. What the plague! can't you produce the money, Fable?

Fable. I cannot indeed, friend.

Trop. Friend! Don't call me your friend—I am not your friend—never will be your friend—never fpeak to you as long as I live.

Bev. Are thefe your leffons of morality, Mr. Fable? Have you reproached me for intemperate indulgence of my paffions, while you were yourfelf practifing deliberated villainy?

Gold. Ah! he has embezzled the money, as fure as I live—Who's here?—Mr. Denier! Your fervant, Sir!

VOL. II.   P   *Enter*

Enter Denier and Capias.

Denier. Your's, Sir. I am forry, Mr. Golding, to have been reduced to the neceffity of taking fo difagreeable a ftep as this may appear to you.

Gold. Difagreeable? not in the leaft difagreeable; I take it rather kind of you, and I am very glad to fee you.

Denier. I am happy to find you confider the matter fo fairly. I had rather have avoided it; but being advifed that it would effentially promote my intereft, and not affect your own, I hope you will excufe it, and indeed rejoice at an opportunity of giving a preference to a friend, inftead of involving him with your common acquaintance.

Gold. Hey-day! what now? Have I loft my fenfes, or every body about me loft theirs? I don't underftand a word you fay, what you mean, or what you drive at.

Capias. My client refers to the bill of Middlefex, taken out againft you, and ferved on you yefterday evening, under which you were arrefted, and are now in Mr. Snap's cuftody.

Gold. I arrefted!—Where is Mr. Snap? Here, houfe!

Enter Snap.

Snap. Did your honour call, Sir?

Gold. Pray, Mr. Snap, did you arreft me laft night?

night?—Did you ferve any writ upon me, Mr. Snap?

Snap. Not I, Sir!—not upon your honour—I arrefted Mr. Golding.

Gold. Mr. Golding!—So it feems I am not come to myfelf again *yet* then!—You, Mr. Sagar, did you help to ferve the writ, friend? [*to Tropick.*

Denier. 'Sdeath, Mr. Capias, there feems to be fome miftake here.

Capias. Truly, there doth appear to have been a wrongful arreft.

Snap. Not at all, Sir.—I knows Mr. Golding well enough—There he ftands! [*pointing to Fable.*] I fhewed him the writ, and he came along with me at once. Did not you, Sir?

Fable. I did—I fubmitted to go with you, thinking it might be of fervice to my friend, and a punifhment to his falfe-hearted creditor.

Trop. This action looks honeftly of old Fable, after all—and yet the money—I don't know what to make of him.

Gold. Nor I neither.

Bev. But Denier's treachery! I could not have believed it!

Gold. No, to be fure!—But you fhall hear of it, Sir, [*to Denier.*] and to your coft too, I promife
you!

you! I'll fue you for damages, and Mr. Fable fhall bring his action for falfe imprifonment—we'll punifh you.

Denier. Indeed! It is time to look about me then —But you had beft have let the bufinefs fleep— I have my revenge in my own hands, I affure you —I have a little packet here——

Gold. Well! what of that, Sir?

Denier. Nay, nothing—only a little news from Bengal.

Gold. Eh!

Denier. Very interefting to a certain lady, not a hundred miles from this place at prefent.

[*Looking at Mrs. Golding.*

Mrs. Gold. How! what's this?

Fable. What does he drive at?

Gold. I wifh he'd be quiet.

Denier. When you have perufed this letter, Mrs. Golding——

Mrs. Gold. Well, Sir!

Denier. You will find, madam——

Gold. Don't believe a word he fays!

Mrs. Gold. You won't let me hear what he fays.

Denier. Poor gentleman! his fears overcome him, but I'll put him out of his pain in an inftant.

This

This letter, madam, arrived it feems by the fame fhips with Mr. Golding, and will inform you, madam, that this grave old gentleman has had a connection in India with another lady——

Mrs. Gold. My hufband!

Gold. [*Afide.*] Oh, plague! I'm betrayed, blown, and undone!

Denier. That this young lady is no other than his daughter——

Mrs. Gold. Lydia!

Denier. That my correfpondent in India, who is his friend, configned her to my family, knowing our connection and acquaintance with your own— and that Mr. Golding himfelf forwarded the late remittance in her favour, meaning to give a colour to an intention he had formed of marrying mifs Lydia to Beverley—All thefe circumftances my correfpondent refers to, as things of courfe in his letter, thinking that Mr. Golding had no objection to my being acquainted with them. Read, read, madam! [*Gives the letter.*

Gold. [*Afide.*] Dead and buried! I wifh I was at Bengal now, or in the black-hole at Calcutta!

Fable. And fo this laft confidence, like every other, you have betrayed, Sir. Is this your vin-dication?

P 3 *Denier.*

Denier. No ; but my revenge, Sir, extorted from me by great provocation——Before you open an account againſt me, ſee that you are able to anſwer all my demands upon you. Take care of the main chance! As to your action at. law, my friend Capias here knows I may deſpiſe it. If the officer has made a falſe arreſt, let the officer anſwer it.—— I have no concern but to take care of myſelf, you know ; ſo come along, Mr. Capias!

Capias. I attend you, Sir. [*Ex. Denier and Capias.*

Bev. Fool that I have been! falſe as my other friends appeared, I ſtill repoſed an entire confidence in his fidelity.

Fable. Sordid, execrable, narrow-minded raſcal!

Mrs. Gold. Here's baſeneſs and treachery! [*After reading the letter.*] Was ever any thing ſo ſcandalous! Concealed children, intrigues in India, and ladies in a corner!

Bev. Well, but, Mrs. Golding——

Mrs. Gold. When he is at home with his family, he is as grave, and dry, and ſober as a judge, forſooth! and yet, when he gets abroad, he can be as gay, and as prodigal, as a young nobleman juſt come to his title and eſtate.

Fable. He may have been to blame, madam; but——

Mrs. Gold. To blame, Mr. Fable! what! thefe were his India voyages then! this was his bufinefs at Bengal! thefe were his large remittances truly! fquandering his fortune, and what was my right, Mr. Fable, upon kept-madams, Eaftern princeffes, black-a-moor harlots, and natural children!

Mrs. Carlt. Nay—don't fay that, Mrs. Golding! mifs Lydia was born in lawful wedlock, I affure you, madam.

Mrs. Gold. What! has he got two wives then?

Mrs. Carlt. No—dear me, madam! mifs Lydia's mother was dead and buried before his marriage with you, madam.

Bev. My Lydia's uneafinefs is infupportable. Shock her no further, I befeech you, madam!

Mrs. Gold. Do you think I have been well treated, Sir?

Bev. The ftory is but new to me, madam; but the main particular is Mr. Golding's firft marriage, which, I apprehend, has been kept fecret merely from the notion of its being difagreeable to your family.

Mrs. Gold. And is this the cafe, Sir?

Gold. It is, indeed—no further harm, I affure you—I fhould have mentioned the affair, to be fure —but——

Enter

Enter Snap.

Snap. Here's one mufter Check below axes for one mufter Fable.

Fable. Oh, defire him to walk up, Sir. Now fet your heart at reft about my conduct, friend.

Trop. You muft make all matters clear then: For at prefent I don't half underftand you.

Fable. Here comes an interpreter.

Enter Check.

Well, Check, have you fettled the bufinefs?

Check. I have, Sir. Mr. Beverley's differences are all paid. I have acquittances from the parties, and the whole account is clofed, Sir.

Bev. Amazement!

Gold. What, is the money gone that way then? None of it embezzled! eh, Check?

Check. Embezzled? Heaven blefs your honour! he has made free to borrow the money left in his hands indeed: But then he has applied all that he could command of his own into the bargain. Embezzled indeed! No, no, Mr. Fable cheats nobody but himfelf, Sir.

Fable. Every particular, Mr. Golding, I am ready to explain. I fhall fay nothing in vindication or apology for my conduct. The motives on which I have acted are obvious,

Trop.

Trop. So they are—fo they are, friend!—Give me your hand, old Fable! give me your hand! I fee you are an honeft fellow at laft, and I am not afhamed to acknowledge you.

Gold. And I am much obliged to you! I have enough and more than enough to ftand the fhock of our affairs, repay you with intereft, and eftablifh our credit; for, thank Heaven, I have been employing my time abroad better than my young partner has done at home.

Mrs. Gold. Oh, you have been very finely employed, to be fure!

Fable. Come, come, this fhould be a day of general happinefs; as an inftance of your univerfal good opinion of me, let me have influence enough to make peace between Mr. and Mrs. Golding; and as an earneft of their reconciliation, let them give their joint confent to unite Lydia and Beverley, and ratify their happinefs!

Bev. Mrs. Golding!—Sir!

Mrs. Gold. What fays her fine papa to it?

Gold. Why, if Lydia——

Mrs. Carlt. Heaven blefs her, fhe dotes on him.

Lydia. Yes, I will own, my dear father, that the change in Mr. Beverley has removed the only objection that I could ever make to him; and I

will

will not blush to confess that the future happiness of my life depends on him.

Fable. Then every thing is adjusted. I give you joy, my friends.

Trop. And I give you joy too. You have puzzled me confoundedly, I confess—I said you were an honest fellow—I knew you were an honest fellow at bottom—but it was a damned long way to the bottom for all that, old Fable.

Fable. My conduct has been mysterious, I confess, friend,—perhaps, in some degree, culpably so—but whenever I puzzled you, be assured I no less embarrassed myself. The least deviation from the straight path is attended with difficulties; and though I have always meant honestly, and thought I acted uprightly, I have had ample reason to experience the convenience and necessity, as well as the beauty, of Truth.

E P I-

EPILOGUE.

Spoken by Mrs. BULKLEY,

WHEN plays are o'er, by Epilogue we're able,
Thro' moral ftrainers, to refine the fable;
Again the field of comedy to glean
From what the author did, or did not mean;
Or, in a gayer mood, on malice bent,
Quite topfy-turvy turn the bard's intent.
Shall we, ye criticks, to-night's play deride?
Or fhall we, ladies, take the milder fide?
Suppofe for once we leave the beaten road,
And try, by turns, the harfh and gentle mode;
A kind of critick country-dance begin;
Right hand and left, crofs over, figure in!
    The critick firft ftrikes off, condemns each fcene,
The tale, the bard, and thus he vents his fpleen:
" While books lie open on each mouldy ftall,
Bills plaifter pofts, fongs paper ev'ry wall,
At ev'ry corner hungry minds may feed,
Wifdom cries out, and he that runs may read.
On learned alms were playwrights ever fed,
And fcraps of poetry their daily bread.

Ev'n

EPILOGUE.

Ev'n Shakefpeare would unthread the novel's maze,
Or build on penny hiftories his plays.
From paltry ballads Rowe extracted Shore,
Which lay like metal buried in the ore.
To jump at once to bards of later days,
What are the riff-raff of our modern plays?
Their native dullnefs all in books intrench;
Mere fcavengers of Latin, Greek, and French,
Sweep up the learned rubbifh, dirt, and duft,
Or from old iron try to file the ruft.
Give me the bard whofe fiery difpofition
Quickens at once, and learns by intuition;
Lifts up his head to think, and, in a minute,
Ideas make a hurly-burly in it;
Struggling for paffage, there ferment and bubble,
And thence run over without further trouble;
'Till out comes play or poem, as they feign
Minerva iffued from her father's brain!
Be all original! ftruck out at once;
Who borrows, toils, or labours, is a dunce:
Genius, alas! is at the loweft ebb;
And none, like fpiders, fpin their own fine web.
What wonder, if with fome fuccefs they ftrive
With wax and honey-to enrich the hive,
If all within their compafs they devour,
And, like the bee, fteal fweets from ev'ry flow'r?

Old

EPILOGUE.

Old books, old plays, old thoughts, will never do:
Originals for me, and fomething new!"
   "New? (cries the lady) Prithee, man, have done!
We know there's nothing new beneath the fun.
Weave, like the fpider, from your proper brains,
And take at laft a cobweb for your pains!
What is invention? 'Tis not thoughts innate;
Each head at firft is but an empty pate.
'Tis but retailing from a wealthy hoard
The thoughts which obfervation long has ftor'd,
Combining images with lucky hit,
Which fenfe and education firft admit;
Who, borrowing little from the common ftore,
Mends what he takes, and from his own adds more,
He is original; or infpiration   ⎫
Never fill'd bard of this, or other nation,   ⎬
And Shakefpeare's art is merely imitation.   ⎭
For 'tis a truth long prov'd beyond all doubt,
Where nothing's in, there's nothing can come out.

   Modes oft may change, and old give way to new.
Or vary betwixt London and Peru;
Yet here, and every where, the general frame
Of nature and of man is ftill the fame:
Huge ruffs and farthingales are out of fafhion;
But ftill the human heart's the feat of paffion:
And he may boaft his genius ftands the teft,
Who paints our paffions and our humours beft.
                                             Cenfure

EPILOGUE.

Censure not all; to praise let all aspire;
For emulation fans the poet's fire.
Put not one grand extinguisher on plays;
But with kind snuffers gently mend their blaze.
While other licenc'd lotteries prevail,
Our bard, by ticklish lott'ry, tempts a sale,
Prints the particulars of his Musæum,
And boldly calls the publick in to see 'em:
Their calculation must his fate reveal,
Who ventures all in the dramatic wheel!

*On account of the length of this Epilogue, many lines
were omitted at the Theatre.*

MAN

MAN AND WIFE;

OR, THE

SHAKESPEARE JUBILEE.

A

COMEDY.

Quid vetat et Nosmet?

*First acted at the Theatre-Royal in Covent-Garden,
on the 7th of October, 1769.*

TO

SIR JOSHUA REYNOLDS, KNT.

PRESIDENT,

OF THE

ROYAL ACADEMY,

THIS COMEDY

IS INSCRIBED

BY HIS ADMIRER,

FRIEND,

AND MOST FAITHFUL

HUMBLE SERVANT,

GEORGE COLMAN.

ADVERTISEMENT.

THE character of Sally (in which the little actress who performed it discovered more than the dawn of theatrical genius) is an imitation of that of Babet, in the comedy of *La Fausse Agnès*, by Destouches; and there are some traits of the character of Kitchen, in the third volume of the Connoisseur.

To these acknowledgments, the author has only to add his most grateful thanks to the publick, for their candid and indulgent reception of this little piece, as well as to the performers, for their great excellence in the representation of it.

PRELUDE.

PRELUDE.

CHARACTERS.

DAPPERWIT,   *Mr. Dyer.*
JENKINS,   *Mr. Hull.*
TOWNLY,   *Mr. Wroughton.*

SCENE, *Covent-Garden.*

Townly crossing the stage. Jenkins calling after him.

Jenkins.

HOLO! Tom!

Townly. Who's there? Jenkins!

Jenk. Ay. Where are you going?

Townly. To the play.

Jenk. The play! what is it? Let me see! [*Looking up at the play-bills.*] MAN and WIFE; or, the SHAKESPEARE JUBILEE. So, so! a new comedy! Whose is it?

Townly. Don't you know?

Jenk. Not I: I have been partridge-shooting ever since the first of September; and am but just come to town. Who is the author?

Townly. Your friend and acquaintance, the manager.

Jenk. What! little Dapperwit?

Q 2

Townly.

PRELUDE.

Townly. The fame. Here he comes, faith! Speak to him, Tom; aſk him about his comedy.

Enter Dapperwit.

Jenk. Ha, George! How do you do?—Well—but you need not look ſo melancholy. What! in mourning? Another annuity, I ſuppoſe: Ha, George?

Dapp. No: I am in mourning, Sir, for a dear and worthy friend, and a moſt valuable partner: A man, whoſe goodneſs of heart was even ſuperior to his admirable talents in his profeſſion.

Townly. Your friend's death was a publick loſs, Sir. He was deſervedly a favourite of the publick, and is very generally regretted.

Jenk. Well, but, George, now you have put on mourning for your friend, I am afraid you will be obliged to continue to wear it for Covent-Garden theatre.

Dapp. I hope not, Sir. The publick is candid and generous; and we muſt be attentive and induſtrious.

Jenk. Yes; you have been dabbling again, I ſee.

Townly. A ſtroke at the Jubilee; ha, Mr. Dapperwit?

Dapp. An innocent laugh, Sir; raiſed out of an adventure,

adventure, which, I have taken the liberty to fuppofe, happened during that period. As to the
Jubilee itfelf, or the defign and conduct of it, I
cannot confider them as objects of fatire.

Townly. No, Sir? They have been roundly
attacked : Lodgings without beds, dinners without
victuals——

Dapp. I know what you mean, Sir. My friend
Pafquin has infinite humour; but his pleafantries
are exceedingly harmlefs, and I believe he wifhes
they fhould be fo.——The fcandal of others is mere
dirt——throw a great deal, and fome of it will ftick.
But the fatire of Pafquin is like fuller's-earth——it
daubs your coat indeed for a time, but it foon
grows dry; and when it rubs off, your coat is fo
much the cleaner.——Thus it has happened on the
prefent occafion——for, after all, gentlemen, if a
building be erected for a particular purpofe, is not
it natural to pull it down again, when that purpofe is anfwered? A great number of people cannot be affembled without creating a croud——a rainy
day will prevent the exhibition of a pageant——and
heavy fhowers deftroy the effect of a firework.

Townly. Ay, Sir; but an ode without poetry——

Dapp. As to the ode——it had one capital fault,
I muft confefs.

Townly and Jenk. Well—and what was it?

Dapp. Why, gentlemen, I underſtood every word of it. Now, an ode, they ſay—an ode—to be very good, ſhould be wholly unintelligible.

Townly. Oh, your ſervant, Sir!

Jenk. Well—but you intend to give it us here, I ſuppoſe?

Dapp. No—the ode can no where be heard to ſo much advantage as from the mouth of the author—and indeed it was ſo happily calculated for the time and place, for which it was originally intended, and the ſpeaker ſo truly felt a noble enthuſiaſm on the occaſion, that you have loſt a very exquiſite pleaſure (never to be retrieved) by not hearing it at Stratford-upon-Avon.

Townly. Well, Sir—but the pageant and the maſquerade—

Dapp. Thoſe you ſhall ſee, Sir—and perhaps they may appear to more advantage, and be ſeen with more ſatisfaction, at the Theatres Royal, than they could have been at Stratford itſelf.

Jenk. Well—but, George—tell us a little of your comedy.

Dapp. Walk in, Sir, and it will ſpeak for itſelf—The curtain is juſt going to draw up.

Jenk. And how do you feel yourſelf?—Eh, George?

Dapp.

Dapp. Much as ufual on fimilar occafions—all hurry and flutter—which ftrangers are apt to miftake for high fpirits, and my friends and acquaintance know to be nothing but apprehenfion.

Townly. We'll give you a hand. I know of a ftrong party againft it, I can tell you, Sir.

Dapp. I fear no party, unlefs my own dullnefs raifes one againft me. The publick will fuffer no party, no malice, to interrupt its amufements. If I fucceed, I fhall owe my fuccefs to their indulgence —if I fail, I fhall owe it to myfelf. With thefe fentiments I enter the theatre. Come, gentlemen —my trial is near coming on, for the play muft be juft going to begin.

Townly. We attend you, Sir.

Jenk. Well faid, little Dapperwit—Have a good heart, my boy! We'll keep it up, I warrant you!

[*Exeunt.*

DRAMATIS

DRAMATIS PERSONÆ.

CROSS,	*Mr. Shuter.*
MARCOURT,	*Mr. Woodward.*
KITCHEN,	*Mr. Dunstall.*
Colonel FRANKLY,	*Mr. Perry.*
Landlord,	*Mr. Morris.*
FLEECE,	*Mr. R. Smith.*
LUKE,	*Mr. Lewes.*
BUCK,	*Mr. Davis.*
SNARL,	*Mr. Wignell.*
Ostler,	*Mr. Quick.*
Men Passengers,	{ *Mr. Herbert,* *Mr. Fox.*

Mrs. CROSS,	*Mrs. Green.*
CHARLOTTE,	*Mrs. Bulkley.*
SALLY,	
LETTICE,	*Mrs. Mattocks.*
Landlady,	*Mrs. Gardner.*
Women Passengers,	{ *Miss Pearce.* *Mrs. Copen.*

Waiters, &c.

MAN

MAN AND WIFE;

OR, THE

SHAKESPEARE JUBILEE.

ACT I.

SCENE, *an Inn at Stratford upon Avon. Bells ringing—People behind calling* Waiter! Waiter! Oftler! Houfe! &c. *Waiters anfwering,* Coming! *Landlady calling. People crofs the ftage different ways—Then enter Landlord and Oftler.*

Landlord.

I TELL you, Oftler, you muft find ftabling for the fet of horfes that came in laft.

Oftler. I tell you, Sir, it is unpoffible: I could not put up the horfes if they would give me ten guineas a ftall for them.

Landlord. Why can't you put fome of them in the corner ftable?

Oftler.

Oſtler. I can't, Sir. Jack Pratt has taken it all for Whirligig, that's entered to run for the Jubalo cup, you know.

Landlord. Well, well—it does not fignify—the gentlemen and ladies are particular acquaintances of the ſteward—and you muſt find room for their horſes ſomewhere.

Oſtler. I muſt turn ſomebody's elſe's horſes to grafs then. 　　　　　　　　　　[*Exit.*

Bells ringing—and people calling again—Waiters anſwering, Coming!—*then enter Luke and three or four other waiters.*

Landlord. Here, waiters, anſwer the bells! I am ſo lame, I can ſcarce hobble about, and I want to be in fifty places at once. Luke, you have the care of moſt part of the houſe : Why don't you anſwer the bells ? 　　　　[*Landlord hobbles out.*

Luke. Coming, Sir, coming!—Here, Richard, take this bottle of Madeira to the gentleman and lady in the As you like it—Jack, carry a crown bowl of punch into the Meaſure for Meaſure—Do you, Thomas, take a dozen more port wine, and pipes and tobacco, to the muſick—they drink like fiſhes —they are in the Tempeſt—d'ye hear ?—and, William, do you make haſte with half-a-dozen of

　　　　　　　　　　　　　　　　claret

claret to the gentlemen in the Merry Wives—they have been calling and ringing this half-hour.

Buck. [*within.*] Waiter!

Luke. Coming, Sir, coming!

Enter Buck, tipsy. [*singing.*]

Buck. All ſhall yield to the mulberry tree;
  Bend to thee,
  Sweet mulberry!
  Matchleſs was he
  Who planted thee,
 And thou like him immortal ſhalt be.

Here, you waiter! you ſcoundrel, you, what's the meaning you don't bring the wine we call'd for? We are obliged to ſit up all night becauſe there are no beds, and you won't ſupply us with liquor to keep us in good humour.

Luke. Beg your honour's pardon—do all in our power to oblige—wait on ſeven companies myſelf; and have ſeven waiters under me, at three and ſixpence a-day.

Buck. How the fellow gabbles!—Have not I ſeen your face before, you Sir?

Luke. Ah—your honour knows me well enough, —I am Luke, Luke, your honour, from the St.
        Alban's.

Alban's. But in the fummer, bufinefs being dead in town—all the quality gone, your honour knows—I go too—and wait at all publick places in the country—I came over here from York races—had half-a-dozen waiters under me there too—A little before that, I was at the inftallation at Cambridge—From hence I go to the Gloucefter mufic-meeting—In October I fhall be at Newmarket—And by the meeting of parliament you'll find Luke, honeft Luke, your honour—at the St. Alban's again.

Buck. Chatter—chatter—chatter—the fellow huddles his words one upon another—and drives 'em out of his mouth like the liquor out of a narrow-necked bottle—Get us the wine directly, you fcoundrel, you.

Luke. Directly, Sir. [*Bell rings.*] Coming, Sir, coming!   [*Exit.*

Enter Snarl, in a night-gown.

Snarl. " And the worft of all beds is a Warwickfhire bed."—Buck! what are you up too?

Buck. Up! I have not been in bed; there was none to be got.

Snarl. I wifh you had had mine then—I had rather fit up without reft, than lie in bed without it.—I have been fwimming in a hammock, with a
                                                                    little

little army walking over me—and as to fleep, one might as well think of it in the Tower of Babel.

Buck. Come along with me then, and we'll teach you how to defpife fleep.—There is a fet of us have taken the room beyond the mufick, for the whole time of the Jubilee—and it ferves us for dining-room, parlour, and bed-chamber. Ever fince dinner to-day—faith, I believe I may fay yefterday, for it is almoft day-light again—we have been following the example fet us at the amphitheatre, and have been drinking bumpers to the immortal memory of Shakefpeare, to the fteward of the Jubilee, with a round of Shakefpeare toafts—Here, old Snarl! here's a Jubilee-favour! fee here! [*fhewing his cockade.*] So, come along with me, my boy, and I'll introduce you to the jollieft company at Stratford upon Avon—for

All fhall yield to the mulberry tree, &c.

[*Exit finging, with Snarl.*

Bar-bell ringing. Landlady (when the bell ceafes) calling, Why, Chambermaid! John Oftler! Boots! Chamberlain! Where are you all?

Then enter Landlady, followed by Colonel Frankly and five other Paffengers in the Birmingham coach.

Landlady. This way! this way, if you pleafe, ladies and gentlemen!—Why, Chambermaid! Richard!

Richard! Thomas! Boots, I fay!—[*Enter Cham-*
bermaid and two or three Waiters.] Here is the
Birmingham coach has been overturned this morning—the gentry frightened out of their wits—and
nobody to fhew them a room, or get them any
refrefhment—D'ye chufe coffee or tea, fome hot
wine and egg, a little warm punch, or a white
negro, ladies and gentlemen?

1ft Man Paff. This is flying, as they fay—flying
to town in one day, as they call it.—Hoifted into
the coach at ten o'clock at night, and ftuck together
as clofe as dried figs—Here, in fpite of fatigue,
we fall afleep before midnight, and foon after
wake with a damned crafh, and find ourfelves
canted into a flough, by way of a feather-bed—
Damn their flying, I fay—a tight fhip with plenty
of fea-room is worth forty on't.

Wom. Paff. I am fure it is a fhame, fo it is, to
ftuff the coach in the manner they do—fix infide
paffengers, two childen in lap—three upon the
box—four upon the top of the coach, and half a
dozen in the bafket—befides hardware parcels and
haunches of venifon in the boot and the coach feats.
Such a load! no wonder the machine fhould break
down or turn over.

Another Wom. Paff. Mercy on me! I am in fuch
a pickle, I am afhamed to be feen—and then I
fhall

ſhall never recover my fright. Pray, ma'am, could you get me a little hartſhorn and water?

Landlady. D'ye hear, Chambermaid? why don't you ſtir?—Some hartſhorn and water for the gentlewoman—fly, I ſay!

2d Man Paſſ. Get me ſome mulled wine and a dry toaſt, d'ye hear, you, Sir?—Zounds, how this houſe is altered! It uſed to be one of the beſt inns upon the road—but now there's hardly getting any body to come near one—no attendance—no accommodation!

Landlady. I hopes the gentry will excuſe all faults at preſent—We never were ſo full in our days—we're almoſt hurried out of our lives—every houſe in the town juſt the ſame—all as buſy as bees about the Jubalo.

2d Man Paſſ. Jubalo! I have heard of nothing but Jubilees, and Shakeſpeares, and mulberry-trees, for theſe three months. What the devil is this Jubilee?

Landlady. Lack-a-day, Sir, I can hardly tell you myſelf; but it is one of the fineſt things that ever was ſeen—There is the great little gentleman from London, and I don't know how many painters, and carpenters, and muſicianers, and actor-people, come down on purpoſe—Great doings, I promiſe you.

1ſt Wom.

1ft Wom. Paff. Is there to be any dancing, pray?

Landlady. Oh, yes—abundance of dancing—but begun with going to church, and finging of *an-tums* and *o-ra-to-ries*, I think they call them—and then there is eating and drinking, and proceffion-ing, and mafquerading, and horfe-racing, and fire-works—So gay—and as merry as the day is long.

1ft Man Paff. And the night too, I warrant you, landlady.

Landlady. Oh, ay; a ball and entertainment, every night, your honour.

[*During this fcene, coffee, tea, &c. handed round to the paffengers.*

Enter Stage-Coachman.

Coachman. The horfes are put to, gentlefolks.

2d Man Paff. By and by—we are coming, mafter Whip!

Coachman. Pleafe to make a little hafte, my ma-fter!—this accident has thrown us quite out of our bias, as I may fay—we fhall be two hours beyond our time before we get to Woodftock to-day—The fly from London will wonder what is become on us.

1ft Man Paff. No, no; they'll think we have broke our necks, or they have broken their own necks, mayhap.

Coachman.

Coachman. Ah, heaven blefs your honour!—you're a merry gentleman.

1ſt Man Paſſ. How many knots d'ye go an hour, brother feaman?

Coachman. We goes above feven miles an hour—near feven and a half—up hill and down, my mafter.

1ſt Man Paſſ. Well—you muſt let out a reef or two this morning, to make up for loſt time—but don't overſet the ſhip again.—But, come—I am purſer to the ſhip's company—what's to pay, mother?

Landlady. Coffee—tea—wine—and bread and butter—five and four-pence, Sir.

1ſt Man Paſſ. There—there's ſix ſhillings.—Good b'wye, mother—I wiſh you a merry Jubalo!

[*Exit Coachman, with Paſſengers.*

Landlady. Kindly welcome, Sir! welcome, ladies! kindly welcome!—[*Bell rings.*] Richard! anſwer to the Magpye! [*Another bell rings.*] Thomas! run up to the Moon!—Chamberlain! [*Exit bawling.*

[*Colonel Frankly left ſitting at table—Re-enter Coachman.*

Coachman. The paſſengers are all in, my maſter!

Frankly. A good journey to them!—I ſhall go

no further with them.—Here's for yourfelf,
honefty!

Coachman. Thank you kindly—heaven blefs you,
mafter!   [*Exit.*

Colonel Frankly alone.

So!—Spite of accidents, I have reached the fcene
of action, however.—Charlotte, I reckon, arrived
yefterday.—Her father and mother both endeavouring to counteract each other, and fhe to baffle
both.—If our plan of operations does but fucceed,
I fhall honour the name of Shakefpeare more than
ever—for to us this celebrity will prove moft truly
a Jubilee.—But who comes here? As I live, that
puppy Marcourt.—The enemy, I fee, is in motion
—but the coxcomb little thinks I am his rival—and,
what is whimfical enough, always chufes to make
me his confidant—tho' I fuppofe he tells me no
more than he tells every body elfe.

Enter Marcourt.

Marc. La Fleur! take the baggage off the chaife,
and come to me immediately.—My dear Frankly!
who would have thought of finding you here?
What brought you to Stratford upon Avon?

Frankly. The Birmingham ftage-coach.

Marc. Oh, ridiculous! And what could cram
you into a ftage-coach?

                                         Frankly.

Frankly. An accident—and another accident had like to have thrown me out of it again.—I have been on a recruiting party in Staffordſhire.—Loſing a wheel of my poſt-chaiſe, about ſix miles off, I was glad to get into the ſtage, which I had ſcarce well done when it was overturned. My fellow-travellers are but juſt ſet forward for London.

Marc. Yes—I met the plebeians juſt as I drove into the yard.—I have been on the road all night myſelf, egad. I rattled through Oxford at mid-night, loud enough to rouſe all the ſleepy fellows of colleges—and am juſt arrived here, where, I find, nobody can get a bed to ſleep in.

Frankly. And what hurried you ſo?

Marc. Why, you muſt know I ſhould have been here laſt night, at furtheſt—but having promiſed to dine at the Macaroni yeſterday with Rocheſter, Brumpton, and Evergreen—

Frankly. The noblemen of thoſe titles, d'ye mean?

Marc. Yes, to be ſure—but you never mention titles—titles of people you live with. 'Tis not the *ton*. When you ſay plain *Townly, Lovelace, Ogleby,* and ſo forth, people who live in the world mean the Duke, Marquis, or Lord of the name;

R 2   but

but when we fay Jack Wilfon, George Belford, Ned Thompfon—and fo on—we mean a commoner. We fpeak of peers as peers fubfcribe themfelves in writing—no chriftian name—and nothing of the title except the place from which it is taken.

Frankly. I beg your pardon. Proceed.

Marc. Why then, being engaged to dine with them, I fay, I did not fet out from Pall-Mall till between eight and nine o'clock.—I loft fix hundred before the chaife came to the door.

Frankly. Deep play!

Marc. Pho! nothing at all. Lovelace loft four and thirty hundred to Jack Airy of the guards, at the fame fitting. We ufed to fet ten or twenty, perhaps, fometime ago—but now, they never make up a *rouleau* of lefs than fifty guineas.—La Fleur! [*calling*] Where is this fellow? I muft get off my boots.

Frankly. Did you ride any part of the way?

Marc. What, in the dark, and on the road?— Oh, no!—Indeed I hardly ever ride now, but in the fpring, through the three parks; or to pay vifits.

Frankly. Vifits on horfeback?

Marc. Why not? We all vifit on horfeback fince the new pavement—and I'm very often out the whole morning without going off the ftones.—

Take

Take horfe at Hall's ftables, a fhort bait at Arthur's
—a flice of pine-apple, and half-a-dozen of fcandal
and politicks at Betty's—and fo make the tour of
the parifh of St. James's, through the fquare, Pall-
Mall, Piccadilly—and Hall's ftables again.—But,
La Fleur! Where the deuce is this fellow? I fha'n't
have my hair drefs'd thefe three hours.

Frankly. Not thefe fix hours, if one may judge
by the quantity.—Is not fo much hair behind troublefome?

Marc. Not at all—So far from it, that above
half of it is falfe—for in an undrefs, unlefs you
have a club as thick as both your doubled-fifts, you
are not fit to be feen—but with that, a little French
hat cut to the quick, that leaves your face as broad
as Harry the Eighth's, an ell of fhirt-fleeves hanging over a fhort half-inch pair of ruffles, a coat
powdered half way down your back, a tambour
waiftcoat, white linen breeches, and a taper fwitch
in your hand, your figure, Frankly, muft be irre-
fiftible.

Frankly. *Your* figure you mean, Marcourt.—But
what could prevail on you to exhibit it at Stratford? Do you intend to make one in the pageant,
and fhew yourfelf as one of the characters of
Shakefpeare?

R 3

Marc.

Marc. No, faith; such an original did not exift in his days; and the writers of our time have left off drawing other peoples' characters for the fake of expofing their own.

Frankly. Well—but your bufinefs here, Marcourt?

Marc. Bufinefs of confequence, I can tell you, Frankly. One muft have a wife, you know, if it is only for the pleafure of getting rid of her.

Frankly. Oh, I conceive you! A matrimonial affair.

Marc. Yes—the old affair with Charlotte.—We have now brought matters to a crifis. Old Crofs and his wife—the father and mother, you know— are always quarreling;—no wonder, therefore, they fquabble about the choice of a hufband for their daughter.—The mother, who is a kind of a coufin of mine, and is defirous of bringing the girl into the world, has pitched upon me.

Frankly. A wife lady!

Marc. Yes—but the tramontane father——

Frankly. Has chofen fome other man, I warrant you.

Marc. He has—but who now, of all mankind, d'ye think is, in his idea, a proper hufband for his daughter? That horrid fellow Kitchen.

Frankly.

Frankly. Kitchen! what, the famous *bon vivant?*

Marc. The fame—a fellow that has not an idea beyond a haunch of venifon. Kitchen and old Crofs are of a club; and when Mrs. Crofs and he have been wrangling, Kitchen, who is reckoned a joker at the club, puts him into humour again.

Frankly. But he has fome real pleafantry, they fay.

Marc. Not he—dull, dull as colonel Grin, who has got Joe Miller by heart, and is always teazing you with a ftory.—No *fplafh* in the world—His converfation is all table-talk, made up of eating and drinking. He is a mere walking larder. His mind is a great pantry, from which he is always ferving up fome choice difhes for the entertainment of his friends and acquaintance.

Frankly. But has not he been able to render himfelf a formidable rival?

Marc. Formidable! ridiculous—no, no—the father is his friend indeed,—but the mother knows reafon—and then the girl is fo fond—poor thing! fhe doats on me to diftraction—pretends to join in old Crofs's defigns in favour of Kitchen, but holds a privy council with the mother and me, and turns every motion to my advantage.—Now, this it is, Frankly, that brings me poft to Stratford.—The

father,

father, you muſt know—but mum! here comes
Kitchen himſelf—I knew we ſhould meet—but I
am prepared for him.—I ſhall ſnap the delicious
morſel out of his mouth, I promiſe him.

Enter Kitchen and Landlord.

Kitchen. What! the gout?—hands and feet,
honeſt Landlord? Your wine is not ſound, I am
afraid.

Landlord. As any in England, Sir.

Kitchen. Well—let me have ſome refreſhment
then—I have met with nothing good upon the
road, ſince the rolls and trout at Uxbridge. Every
where elſe, plague take them, they gave me nothing but cow beef, ram mutton, red veal, ſtale
eggs, and white bacon.

Landlord. You will find the beſt of every thing
here, Sir.—We never hear any complaints—and
at preſent we have made large proviſions on account of the Jubilee.

Kitchen. So you had need, Landlord; for you
ſeem to have an army to eat them up.

Marc. Prithee, Landlord, what is this Jubilee?
—Mr. Kitchen, your humble ſervant.

Kitchen. Your ſervant, Sir. [*Diſtant civility on
both ſides—conceitedly on the part of Marcourt, and
rough on that of Kitchen.*

Landlord.

Landlord. The Jubilee, Sir, is on account of our famous townſman, Shakeſpeare—the great play-writer, that wrote King Lear and his three daugh-ters, and Othello Moor of Venice. They ſay he loved veniſon—and, Heaven bleſs him! he has ſet many a haunch going in our houſe—the town is brim-full of company.

Marc. If it is a Jubilee, it muſt be nonſenſical.—I was at the Jubilee at Rome ſome years ago.

Landlord. Oh, this is quite another thing, I be-lieve, Sir. There is no popery in our Jubilee, though it began with going to church, they ſay.

Kitchen. I never knew any of our travelled fine gentlemen that did not draw compariſons between things totally oppoſite. Between antient Rome and this country, there might be ſome reſemblance; but modern Italy is no more to be compared to Old England, than a ſirloin of beef to a ſpoonful of macaroni.

Marc. How ſhould a man talk of things abroad, who has paſt his whole life at home? You will allow us, Mr. Kitchen, to be more competent judges, who have travelled, and ſkimmed the cream of Europe.

Kitchen. I can travel to more advantage than moſt of you, without ſtirring out of my elbow-chair.—I can digeſt what I read, and chew the

cud

cud of reflection upon it.—As for you fine gentlemen, you skim the cream of Europe, as you fay,
and bring home nothing but froth, and whipt-
fillabub.

Marc. Well faid, John Bull!—You like Shakefpeare now, I warrant you?

Kitchen. Like him? I adore him! No man of
fenfe, and true tafte can do otherwife.

Marc. Ay, I thought fo. You prefer his puns
and quibbles to the wit and humour of Moliere, I
fuppofe.

Kitchen. No, Sir.—Bigotry is not the growth of
this country, in literature any more than religion.
Puns and quibbles were the vicious tafte of the
times; and if they made their way into the pulpit,
no wonder that they were to be met with on the
ftage. I hate a forced chafe of puns and little
conceits, as much as you can do.—Sheer wit is
like fheer wine—but a pun or a quibble—rot it—
a pun is nothing but gingling the glaffes.

Marc. Oh! they are not the only faults of his
barbarous farces—as uncouth a medley to prefent
to this age as a pageant or a puppet-fhow.—No
foreigner can endure him.

Kitchen. They can't tafte him, becaufe they don't
underftand him.

Marc. They can underftand him well enough
to

to be fhocked at his abfurdities. A baby in the firft act become a grown perfon in the laft—plays made out of halfpenny ballads—ghofts and grave-diggers, witches and hobgoblins! Brutus and Caffius converfing like a couple of Englifh common-councilmen—Hamlet killing a rat—and Othello raving about an old pocket-handkerchief.—There's your Shakefpeare for you!

Kitchen. Now I fhould have been fure you had travelled, if I had not known it before. This is a mere hafh of foreign criticifm, as falfe as fuperficial, and made up of envy and ignorance.—Shakefpeare, Mr. Marcourt—Shakefpeare is the turtle of literature. The lean of him may perhaps be worfe than the lean of any other meat;—but there is a deal of green fat, which is the moft delicious ftuff in the world.

Frankly. Indeed, Marcourt, I think the gentleman is too hard for you.

Kitchen. A cruft for the criticks! that's all.

Marc. Never mind it. I fhall be too hard for him prefently.

Kitchen. I underftand you—but I don't believe it. Charlotte has no tafte for foreign cookery.

Marc. Then fhe has lefs tafte than I imagine—The family are now at Stratford.—Where do they lodge, Landlord?

Landlord.

Landlord. Whom does your honour mean?

Marc. Mr. Crofs and his family.

Landlord. They have taken a whole houfe near the new hall, Sir.

Marc. I'll tell you what, Mr. Kitchen—I'll give you a hundred pounds to receive a thoufand on my marriage with Charlotte.

Kitchen. With all my heart; and I'll lay you a hogfhead of claret you never marry her at all.

Marc. Done.

Kitchen. And done again.—And if you have a mind for any other bet, this gentleman fhall hold the ftakes.

Frankly. Have a care I don't run away with them!

Kitchen. Never fear!

Marc. Come then!—firft to drefs, and then for the Signora!

Kitchen. And I fay, firft for a little refrefhment. —Ceres and Bacchus are the warmeft friends of Venus.—I never found that love took away my ftomach.   [*Exeunt feverally.*

A C T

A C T II.

SCENE, *an apartment in Crofs's houfe—Mr. and Mrs. Crofs at breakfaft. They fit filent fome time.*

Crofs.

WELL! am I to have another difh of tea or no, Mrs. Crofs?

Mrs. Crofs. Lord, Mr. Crofs! I wonder you did not find fault that I had not poured out the fecond difh before you drank the firft!

Crofs. Pfhaw! [*throwing a flice of bread and butter on the plate.*

Mrs. Crofs. What's the matter now, Mr. Crofs?

Crofs. Matter!—the bread's bad—the butter's rank—and the tea as coarfe as chopt hay.—It's a ftrange thing one can never have a comfortable breakfaft!

Mrs. Crofs. There is no fuch thing as comfort, wherever you are. The bread is as good bread as ever was tafted—the butter's as fweet as a violet—and the tea is the beft fixteen-fhilling green in the world; but in town it's juft the fame thing— you do nothing but find fault there too—though

I have

I have my fugar from Fenchurch-ftreet—my tea.
from the Grafshopper—and the beft Epping-butter
from the corner of Savile-row.

Crofs. Ay; you have your particular place for
every thing—Not becaufe it's better, but becaufe
it's the fafhion. You would fooner give a crown a
yard more for a filk than buy it any where but on
Ludgate-Hill—But I am never in the right in any
thing—I dare fay now you will infift upon it, that
this room is not damp—though I can fwear it was
not dry when I came down this morning—I fhall
catch my death of cold, I fuppofe.

Mrs. Crofs. Lord!—you're fo delicate—You may
think yourfelf very well off to have a good houfe
over your head, when fo many people are glad to
lie in a hayloft, and to lodge their fervants in lan-
daus and poft-chaifes.

Crofs. Well, it's no matter—I deferve it—what
the plague had I to do at Stratford ?—Such a ridiculous journey! I wonder how I could be fuch a
blockhead as to give into it—And as for yourfelf
too, you care no more for Shakefpeare, than I for
the pope of Rome.

Mrs. Crofs. And what does that fignify, as to
going to the Jubilee ? Are not all the people of condition round the country to be here ? Shakefpeare

. is

is nothing to the purpofe; I would not fee the fineft play the man ever wrote but in a fide-box —And one only goes into the fide-box, becaufe it's going into the beft company.

Crofs. Yes, that's reafon enough for you to do any thing—Becaufe a countefs, who has a range of rooms as long as Pall-Mall, gets the whole town together at her route—You muft have a route too, and fqueeze all your acquaintance into two clofets and a cupboard—Nay, laft winter, when the town ran mafquerade-mad, you got a ridiculous party of about eighteen or twenty fops and flirts, to make fools of themfelves, and called it a mafquerade.

Mrs. Crofs. I am fure every body admired the ftile of the illumination—and then neither Negri nor Robinfon ever fet out a more elegant fide-board —Lady Frankair called it Mrs. Cornelys' in miniature—But you have no notion of any thing that's genteel—You are not fit to live among the world.

Crofs. The world! zounds, madam, does your map of the world comprehend only two parifhes? —The inhabitants of which laugh at all the reft for aping them!—Don't you fee that this narrow circle that you call *the world*, defpife all you that are out of it, and want to force your way into

it?

it? Are not they perpetually running away from you? And are not they carrying London to Hampſtead and Highgate, on purpoſe to get rid of you?

Mrs. Croſs. This is all mere ſcandal and malice—It is very well known that I ſee none but the firſt people—And if you had not affronted Sir Peter Levee, he would have engaged to make Charlotte a maid of honour.

Croſs. And I'll make her what moſt maids of honour would wiſh to be—The wife of a man of good ſenſe, with a handſome fortune.

Mrs. Croſs. Not of Mr. Kitchen, I hope.

Croſs. And why not Mr. Kitchen, madam?

Mrs. Croſs. He had better marry his cook-maid—a wretch!—He never mixes with a perſon of faſhion, except by chance at Bath, where he goes to recover his digeſtion after having over-eat himſelf.

Croſs. And that flimſy piece of quality-binding, Marcourt, is always running after a title, like a child after a butterfly—He is a mere lord-hunter, and loſes all the little ſenſe and money he has in the purſuit.

Mrs. Croſs. Nobody deſpiſes good company, but thoſe that have not accompliſhments to qualify themſelves to get into it. Mr. Marcourt ſees every body—

body—fubfcribes to Almack's, and (the firft vacant borough) my lord Neverout will bring him into parliament.

Crofs. With all my heart; fo as the puppy does not put himfelf up as a candidate for my daughter.

Mrs. Crofs. I am fure, if ever fhe has any thing to fay to that Mr. Kitchen, fhe deferves to be confined for a mad woman.

Crofs. There are a great many mad women, that are not confined at all.

Mrs. Crofs. And there is fuch a thing as a melancholy mad man, who is of all others, the moft miferable in himfelf, and the moft fhocking to other people.

Crofs. Don't provoke me, Mrs. Crofs! don't provoke me! You know I can't bear it.

Mrs. Crofs. What's the matter with the man? Have I faid a fingle thing to give you the leaft provocation? I won't fpeak another word.

[*They fit filent a little while.*

Crofs. A puppy! [*muttering.*
Mrs. Crofs. Ti tum dum! [*humming.*
Crofs. A coxcombical fellow that— [*muttering.*
Mrs. Crofs. Li tum ti—— [*humming.*
Crofs. A provoking woman!
Mrs. Crofs. Tum ti tum tee—— [*humming.*
Crofs. Zounds! there's no bearing this ufage—

I have a good mind to order the chaife, and fet out for London immediately.

Mrs. Crofs. Lord, Mr. Crofs, why do you put yourfelf fo much out of temper? am not I as quiet as a lamb?

Crofs. You know—you know, Mrs. Crofs, that this cool infolence is ten times more provoking than paffion—But I'll fay no more to you—I am a fool to mind your nonfenfe. [*takes a paper and reads.*

Mrs. Crofs. [*after a little while.*] Will you have any more tea, Mr. Crofs?

Crofs. No.   [*without looking off the paper.*

Mrs. Crofs. Shall I fend away the things?

Crofs. Pfhaw!   [*turns round in his chair.*

Mrs. Crofs. John! [*Servant enters.*] take away the tea-things!

Crofs. Let them alone!

Mrs. Crofs. Why, have not you done breakfaft, Mr. Crofs?

Crofs. No.

Servant. Mr. Kitchen, Sir, is juft come to wait on you.

Mrs. Crofs. Pho!

Crofs. Mr. Kitchen! Shew him up immediately! [*Exit Servant—Mrs. Crofs following.*] Stay, madam! I infift upon your not leaving the room.

Mrs.

Mrs. Crofs. What fhould I ftay for? I have nothing to fay to him.

Crofs. I don't care—I won't have him affronted.
[*Mrs. Crofs throws herfelf into a chair.*

Enter Kitchen.

Crofs. My dear friend!

Kitchen. Sir, I am heartily glad to fee you—Madam, your moft humble fervant!
[*to Mrs. Crofs.*

Mrs. Crofs. Your fervant, Sir. [*Pouting.*

Crofs. Well—but where's your fervant and your portmanteau?

Kitchen. At the White Lion.

Crofs. Oh, you muft order them here—you muft be with us during the Jubilee; we have a very good room for you.

Re-enter Servant.

Servant. Mr. Marcourt, madam, is come to wait on you.

Mrs. Crofs. Oh, I am glad of it—fhew him into my dreffing-room; I'll wait on him there—Mr. Kitchen, your humble fervant. [*Exit haftily.*

Kitchen. Your fervant, madam.

Crofs. Harkye, John!

Servant.

Servant. [*Returning.*] Sir!

Crofs. Tell my daughter Charlotte to come here.

Servant. Yes, Sir.   [*Exit.*

Kitchen. Well, Sir, I have obeyed your orders, you fee.—I have croffed the country from the Weft of England, on purpofe to attend you.— Colonel Cramwell, Lord Pepper, and two or three more of us, have been on a coafting party.—It has been a delightful fummer; and I think I never knew the whitings, turbots, brills, red mullets, and John Dories, in higher perfection.

Crofs. I am moft heartily glad to fee you, Mr. Kitchen; and this meeting will, I think, be deci- five.—Our fchemes are now ripe for execution. I have humoured my wife in this ridiculous jour- ney, merely becaufe it gave me a better opportunity of thwarting her in the grand point of Charlotte's marriage.—This houfe, you muft know, has been taken in our name for this month, under the pre- tence of attending this Jubilee—but *really* in order to make the family parifhioners—by which means the banns have been afked, as the law requires, between you and Charlotte—and the minifter is prepared to perform the ceremony this very morn- ing.

Kitchen. But is Mifs Charlotte prepared for it?

                                                      Crofs.

Crofs. Perfectly—Charlotte is a fhrewd clever girl; and tho'. fhe carries it fair with her mother, will do every thing that I bid her, and is wholly in your intereft.—Oh, here fhe is!

Enter Charlotte.

Come hither, Charlotte! I have once more the pleafure of prefenting Mr. Kitchen to you, and by and by I hope you will receive him as my fon-in-law.

Charl. Don't you think, Sir, I have a hard tafk of it between you and my mama? Your commands are as oppofite as North and South, and yet you both expect to be obeyed.

Crofs. Never tell me—I am mafter of the family —it is her duty to honour and obey; and I am refolved to be abfolute.

Charl. Ah, my dear papa! your infifting fo eternally upon your right, is the very thing that renders it fo difficult to maintain it. All women love power; and the beft way of fecuring their obedience, is to tell them that they govern you.

Crofs. Did not I fay, fhe was a fhrewd girl, Mr. Kitchen?

Kitchen. The young lady is perfectly in the right. A wife is like a trout; fhe muft be tickled, Mr. Crofs.

Crofs.

Crofs. Well—but have you prepared matters? How do you propofe to manage it?

Charl. Juft as I have managed every thing elfe : while my mama fuppofes I approve of *her* choice, fhe has no fufpicion of my favouring your own— but what d'ye think fhe would fay, if I was to tell her that Mr. Marcourt was my averfion?—I have never dropt a fingle word to her in behalf of Mr. Kitchen.

Crofs. Well, well—that may be right enough, perhaps.—But no wonder that Marcourt's your averfion. He's one of the moft empty, featherheaded coxcombs in town.

Kitchen. An infipid fellow, madam!—neither pepper nor falt in him.

Crofs. True. My daughter has not the leaft relifh for him.—But, Charlotte! won't it be difficult to carry on this affair in the midft of fo much company?

Charl. Oh no! the more the merrier, Sir.

Kitchen. But the fewer the better chear, madam.

Charl. Not in this inftance, Sir. This Jubilee is a fortunate circumftance. One is never fo private as in a croud, you know.

Kitchen. Why, that's true. Intrigues carried on in the face of the world are always leaft liable to

detection

detection—and now-a-days moſt people ſeem to act upon that principle.

Charl. A truce with your ſatire, Sir ; for we are not to act barefaced, I aſſure you : and the Jubilee concluding with a maſquerade affords us an admirable opportunity—Do you—Lord, I'm a mad girl —I was going to make an aſſignation with you before my father's face.

Croſs. Do! do—I inſiſt on it.

Charl. Why then, I ſhall ſlip on my dreſs, which is a blue Turkiſh habit, directly after dinner, and in that I ſhall expect you about ſeven o'clock.

Kitchen. I am a Turk, if I do not attend you.

Charl. Take care I don't find you a baſhaw.

Kitchen. A downright Engliſh huſband, I promiſe you.—No water-drinking religion for me, madam ; I ſhall break the laws of Mahomet this very evening, and toaſt your health in a bumper of the moſt generous wine to be found in the town of Stratford.

Croſs. Temperance! temperance 'till after to-morrow, I beſeech you, Mr. Kitchen! After that, you may drink up the Avon.

Kitchen. I would not give a guinea a ton for it —Shakeſpeare upon the banks, and the perch out of the ſtream, are all I want of it.

Croſs.

Cross. But come—we muft bid Charlotte good-morrow—I'll attend you to the inn, and order your fervant and baggage up hither.

Charl. What will mama fay to that?

Cross. I don't care what fhe fays; I will have it fo.

Charl. How! relapfing already, papa? Mama muft not be made uneafy, for many reafons—fo don't be angry or jealous if I take very little notice of you to-day, Mr. Kitchen.

Kitchen. No! but, to-morrow morning—ay, and to-morrow evening—Oh, that the doctor had but faid grace! The very thought creates an appetite.

> [*Exeunt Cross and Kitchen.*

Charlotte alone.

Charl. I don't know a young lady with more bufinefs upon her hands than myfelf. My father and his friend to treat with on one hand, my mother and her dainty quater-coufin to negotiate with on the other—and all the while, like a true minifter, to attend to nothing but my own feparate intereft! It puts me in mind of fome of the road-pofts I faw upon our journey, pointing three ways at once.

Lett. [*Peeping in.*] Is the coaft clear?

Charl.

Charl. I am all alone. What's the matter, Lettice?

Lett. Only a letter from Colonel Frankly.

Charl. He is arrived, I hope.

Lett. Safe arrived, madam. He is at the White Lion.

Charl. But where is the letter!

Lett. Blefs me! I have not loft it fure—oh, no! here it is, ma'am!—[*gives the letter, which Charlotte reads while Lettice is talking.*] Ah, you may take your leave of love-letters now. Marriage makes a wonderful alteration in ftile and fentiment.—The letters of married people are like your papa's and mama's converfation.

Charl. Well—I hope nobody faw it delivered to you?

Lett. Nobody but your fifter Sally. Ah, fhe's a fly little urchin! tho' fhe is but a few years younger than you, fhe has cut all her eye-teeth, I affure you, madam. She afked me, if that was not colonel Frankly's livery—and then fhe looked as cunning and roguifh—fhe knows what's what, I promife you, madam.—Here the little romp comes.

Enter

Enter Sally, running.

Sally. Oh fifter, fifter! I am come to give you joy, fifter.

Charl. Joy! of what, my dear?

Sally. Colonel Frankly is arrived, fifter!

Charl. Well! and what's that to me? why fhould you wifh me joy upon that account?

Sally. Oh, I know why well enough—I am no more a fool than my elder fifter.

Charl. What does the child mean?

Sally. Child indeed! you were no fimpleton at my age, I warrant you, fifter.

Charl. And what then?

Sally. Come, come! I fee you are afraid of me—but you need not, I promife you—and I fhall have ten times more pleafure in helping you out, than I could poffibly have in telling papa and mama.

Lett. Ah! you're a rare one! you'll make a fine young lady one of thefe days, I warrant you.

Sally. You truft Lettice here, I know well enough; and you had better truft me too, I can tell you, fifter. Nay, fuppofing I could do you no good, it is in my power to do you a great deal of mifchief.

Charl. What! do you threaten me, then?

Sally. No, indeed and indeed, I don't, fifter. If

I knew

I knew all your secrets, I would not hurt you for the world.

Lett. And will you be a good little girl now—and tell nobody—and do every thing we bid you?

Sally. That I will—Tell me all, and if I tell papa or mama, or any body else, I wish I may die, sister!

Lett. E'en tell her, ma'am! She loves a little roguery to her heart—and then she is such an arch little soul, I think she may be of use—I have cut out some business for her already.

Sally. I am glad of it—For goodness-sake, let me know it—I'll play my part as well as any of you.

Lett. Ay, I'll be bound for you.

Sally. Well—Colonel Frankly is a charming man, to be sure—and as my elder sister has a colonel, I think I have a right to a captain.

Charl. Hush, my dear; you will be overheard by the family.

Sally. No, I sha'n't—Papa is just gone out with Mr. Kitchen, and mama is in her dressing-room with Mr. Marcourt. She desires to see you there as soon as the procession is over.

Charl. I know her business, and can scarce bear the thoughts of it. How disagreeable it is to live in a state of perpetual dissimulation with both my parents!

Lett.

Lett. Never mind it, · ma'am! never mind it!—It is entirely their own faults. They have each of them encouraged and advifed you to practife deceit; and neither of them can blame you for following their inftructions.

Charl. Ah, Lettice, it is a poor apology for our faults, to excufe them by thofe of other people.

Lett. Their conduct is an excufe for every thing.—They advife you to diffemble to bring their fchemes to bear—and you take their advice in order to compafs you own.

Sally. But come, Lettice—Why don't you tell me what I am to do? I long to be bufy.

Lett. We may be interrupted here. Come into your fifter's room—You muft tell a little fib or two.

Sally. Oh, let me alone! I fhall not be at a lofs for that, I warrant you.—Lord, how grave you look, fifter!

Charl. My dear, don't you think I have fome reafon?

Sally. Reafon! no indeed—Are not you going to be married?—Well, you eldeft daughters have a fine time of it, to take place of your younger fifters in every thing—but no matter—I fhall grow older and older every day, you know.

Charl. Go, you little madcap!

Sally.

Sally. I fhall dance at your wedding, I promife you.

Lett. Hold your tongue, you little devil you!

Sally. [*Singing.*]
Well, well, fay no more!
Sure you told me before,
I prithee, go talk to your parrot, your parrot;
I'm not fuch an elf,
Tho' I fay it myfelf,
But I know a fheep's head from a carrot, a carrot!
[*Exeunt.*

SCENE,

SCENE, *a street in Stratford; on one side, the house wherein Shakespeare was born.*

The PAGEANT,
Exhibiting the characters of Shakespeare.

Martial Musick.

ROMAN CHARACTERS.

Soldiers——two by two.
Fasces.
Trophies——S. P. Q. R. &c.

CORIOLANUS.
Roman Ladies——dishevelled.

JULIUS CÆSAR.
The Roman Eagle.
Brutus and Cassius——bearing daggers.

Soft Musick.

ANTONY and CLEOPATRA.
Charmion and Iras.

Grand

Grand Mufick.

OLD ENGLISH CHARACTERS.

KING JOHN.
Conftance, Prince Arthur, and Hubert.

· RICHARD the THIRD.
Edward the Sixth——and duke of York.

HARRY the EIGHTH.
Cardinal Wolfey.

Coronation Anthem.

Anne Bullen under coronation canopy.
Attendants.

Magical Mufick, " *Above, about, and underneath.*"
PROSPERO.
Miranda and Ferdinaud.
Drunken Sailors.
Trinculo and Caliban.
Ariel.
Dæmons and other Spirits.

Macbeth's Mufick.
HECATE.
Witches——two by two.
The two Baby Spirits.——One with a crown,
the other with a bough.

Fairy

Fairy Muſick.

OBERON and TITANIA——in a nutſhell.
Other Fairies.

Solemn Muſick.

The TRAGICK MUSE.

OTHELLO and DESDEMONA.

GHOST in HAMLET.
Hamlet, following the Ghoſt, with his ſword drawn.
Ophelia in her madneſs.

LEAR and CORDELIA.

JACHIMO.
POSTHUMUS and IMOGEN.
Bellarius between the two brothers.

MACBETH, with daggers bloody.
Banquo's Ghoſt.
Lady Macbeth, with the candle.

FRIAR LAWRENCE.

Dead march in Saul.

Juliet's bier.   Attendants.

Allegro.

Allegro.

The COMICK MUSE.

Shallow and Silence.
Slender and Dr. Caius.
Ford, Sir Hugh Evans, and Page.
Mrs. Quickly and Piftol.
Bardolph and Nym.
Mrs. Ford, Falftaff, and Mrs. Page.

TOUCHSTONE and LANCELOT.

MALVOLIO, crofs-gartered.

Andante.

FLORIZEL and PERDITA.
Autolicus.

ANTONIO and BASSANIO.
Portia and Neriffa (as Lawyers).
Shylock—with knife, fcales, and bond.

Flourish.

DRAMATICK TROPHIES.
PEGASUS.
APOLLO.

The Car (drawn by the Mufes) containing the
Buft of SHAKESPEARE, crowned by
TIME and FAME,
And attended by the THREE GRACES.
Cupids, Satyrs, Bacchanals, &c.

AIR. By Mrs. MATTOCKS.

I.

Sweeteft Bard that ever fung,
  Nature's glory, Fancy's child;
Never fure did witching tongue,
  Warble forth fuch wood-notes wild!

II.

Come each Mufe, and fifter Grace,
  Loves and Pleafures, hither come;
Well you know this happy place:
  Avon's banks were once your home.

III.

Bring the laurel, bring the flow'rs,
  Songs of triumph to him raife!
He united all your pow'rs,
  All uniting, fing his praife!

Ode on Dedicating a Building to Shakefpeare.

ACT

ACT III.

*Charlotte and Sally meeting Lettice.—Charlotte in a
pink domino—Lettice in a blue Turkish habit.*

Lettice.

WELL! have you been with your mama
and Mr. Marcourt, madam?

Charl. I have.

Lett. And what have you done?

Charl. Told them every thing that paſt between
me and my papa.

Lett. Indeed!

Charl. To be ſure. I have done ſo all along,
you know; and this has inſpired ſo much confidence on each ſide, that neither one nor the other
entertain the leaſt ſuſpicion of my deceiving them
both.

Lett. But how have you ſettled matters, madam?

Charl. I think, very cleverly. Mr. Marcourt
has ſuggeſted to my mama, that that there is nothing ſo much like a perſon of faſhion, as to receive

maſks at your own houſe before going to the publick maſquerade: So our doors are to be thrown
open to all Stratford. You are (as we ſettled at
firſt) to amuſe Mr. Kitchen in that habit; and I
am, as my mama ſuppoſes, to go off with Mr.
Marcourt in this.

Lett. But your mama will find herſelf ſadly deceived.

Sally. Yes; I am to manage that, Lettice. My
ſiſter has given me my cue—and never truſt me,
if I don't make a fool of him.

Lett. Oh, I don't doubt you.

Charl. All we want at preſent is a little time,
Lettice. Colonel Frankly, you may be ſure, will
be here. The other parties muſt be put upon a
wrong ſcent, and in the mean while I ſhall give
my hand to the colonel, which my papa and mama
have ſeverally deſtined to Mr. Marcourt and Mr.
Kitchen.

Lett. But how am I to treat Mr. Kitchen?

Charl. Why thus—Ha! yonder comes Mr.
Marcourt. Come into the next room, Lettice,
and I'll explain every thing—Now remember your
inſtructions, Sally! -

Sally. Let me alone! go, and give Lettice her
leſſon: I am perfect in mine.

Lett.

Lett. Ay, you are an apt fcholar, I'll warrant you.

Charl. Well! fuccefs attend you! Come, Lettice!

[*Exeunt Charl. and Lett.*

Sally alone.

Sally. Now for as many fibs as I ever told my mama or my governefs! Here the gentleman comes —full of pride and conceit. He is a pretty man too; but I don't like him half fo well as colonel Frankly.

Enter Marcourt.

Marc. Ha! my little puppet! what do you do here all alone, my dear?

Sally. Nothing at all, not I, Sir.

Marc. You feem dull, my dear. Come, let us chatter a little, and that will put you in fpirits.

Sally. Will it? why, what will you fay to me, Sir?

Marc. Say to you? I'll tell you you're as handfome as a little angel.

Sally. Ah! but do you really believe fo, Sir?

Marc. Yes, indeed do I—I could almoft find in my heart to make love to you.

Sally. Oh, but they fay I am too little yet awhile —but have a little patience, and I fhall be as tall as my fifter.

Marc. That you will very foon, my little dear!

and

and when I am married to your fister, I'll take care to get you a hufband.

Sally. Oh dear! you married to my fifter! When will that be, I wonder?

Marc. Very foon, my dear! to-day, or to-morrow, perhaps.

Sally. To-morrow come-never, I believe.

Marc. Why fo, my dear?

Sally. Ah, you want to pump me. But I muft not tell tales, you know. I fhall be buffed if I do,

Marc. Egad, I may be tricked here—[*Afide.*] Well, but, my little dear, you may tell *me*—You fhall come to no harm, I promife you.

Sally. And won't you fay that I told you?

Marc. No: I'll fwear——

Sally. Oh dear! don't you fwear: that's naughty, and will frighten me.

Marc. Well—upon my honour then, nobody fhall know that you told me.

Sally. But is there nobody liftening?

Marc. Not a creature—we're all alone—Come now! hide nothing from me; there's a good little foul!

Sally. Why then—you are impofed upon, Sir.

Marc. Ay? egad, I was afraid fo—but how? how, my dear?

Sally.

Sally. As they think I am but a child, they don't mind what they fay before me—fo I hear all their contrivances.

Marc. Well! what are they?

Sally. It made me mad to think they fhould abufe fuch a charming pretty gentleman, as you are. I am fure, if I was my fifter, I fhould like you a thoufand times better than Mr. Kitchen.

Marc. What a fenfible little creature it is!— There's a good child!—but what were the contrivances you were fpeaking of?

Sally. For my fifter to go off with Mr. Kitchen, and be married to him.

Marc. Ay! how?

Sally. In a blue Turkifh habit.

Marc. Oh, I know that.

Sally. No, indeed, but you don't, Sir. I know what you think well enough. I heard my fifter fay that fhe had fairly told mama and you, that fhe had fettled it fo with papa, only to throw you the more off your guard, and make you believe fhe would go along with you in a pink domino. I pretended to be for Mr. Marcourt, fays fhe: But indeed, fays fhe, I fhall do as my papa would have me, for all that. I'll put on the blue Turkifh habit, and go with Mr. Kitchen.

Marc. So, fo! I am to be bubbled then.

T 4

Sally.

Sally. That you will, if you don't look after the lady in the Turkish habit, I can tell you, Sir.

Marc. Oh, I shall take care, I warrant you.

Sally. Ay, you know all their secrets now; but if you say I told you, I'll never let you know any thing again.

Marc. Never fear, my dear.—I'll blow up all their plots, and pretend I discovered them by accident.

Sally. Do, do!—But I must leave you now, Sir; for if my sister, or papa, or Lettice, should see us together, they may suspect something.

Marc. So they may—but before you go, let me give you one kiss for your intelligence!

Sally. Oh, no! I must not kiss the gentlemen.

Marc. Go, you little coquet, you!

Sally. However, I'll make you one of my best dancing curtsies.

Marc. Oh, your servant, miss!

[*She makes him a low curtsy—but as he turns away, holds up her hands and laughs at him—He turns suddenly towards her—she calls up a grave look, makes him another low curtsy, and runs away romping.*

Marcourt alone.

A lucky discovery this—and very whimsically made too—Fools and children always speak truth, they

they fay—But Charlotte cannot ferioufly prefer Kitchen to me—I think I may venture to fay that's impoffible—No! She has given into this, merely to oblige her father, and will be happy to fee his intentions defeated. I'll about it inftantly—It fhall be done, my dear, on purpofe to oblige you. [*Exit.*

A hall.

Enter Mrs. Crofs and Lettice.

Mrs. Crofs. Well, I declare I am quite delighted with this idea of Mr. Marcourt's, of receiving mafks at home. It is fo much in the ftile of people of condition—The gentility of it pleafes me almoft as much as contradicting my hufband.

Lett. It is a great happinefs that mafquerades are coming into fafhion again. It gives a lady a fine opportunity of having her own way, to be fure, ma'am.

Mrs. Crofs. So it does, Lettice, as Mr. Crofs fhall experience. Charlotte has followed my directions, I hope?

Lett. To a tittle, ma'am—You fee I am ready drefs'd for the purpofe.

Mrs. Crofs. Very well. I fhall have witnefles of my triumph too—That will be charming. Is every thing ready in the apartments to receive the company?

Lett.

Lett. Every thing, ma'am.

Mrs. Crofs. Have they moved the partition between the fore and back room?

Lett. They have, ma'am.

Mrs. Crofs. Have they ftuck the ends of *fpermaceti* in the girandoles? And have you fent to the apothecary's for a fufficient quantity of cream of tartar to make lemonade?

Lett. Your orders have been exactly obeyed, ma'am.

Mrs. Crofs. Mighty well. You know I die, if I have not every thing in the higheft ftile—If I give but a plate of bread and butter, I give it like a perfon of condition. But I muft go, and do the honours of the houfe—I fee fome mafks going into the yellow room—I have fent cards to every body one knows that's at Stratford—And I expect a member of parliament with his wife and daughters, the dowager lady Codille, Sir Thomas Frippery, and a Yellow admiral—Be fure you take care, Lettice!   [*Exit.*

Lettice alone.

Lett. Yes; I fhall take care of more than you are aware, I promife you, madam—How happy the old gentlewoman makes herfelf, in her fuccefs, as fhe fancies it! My mafter is in the very fame cafe—

cafe—And my young lady too much for them both. Surely, there muſt be ſome very extraordinary pleaſure in a man's plaguing his wife, and a woman's tormenting her huſband. My maſter and miſtreſs think of nothing elſe. They are like flint and ſteel, perpetually ſtriking fire out of each other—Oh, here comes Mr. Kitchen—As true to his appointment, as if it was an invitation to turtle or veniſon —Now for a little maſquerade frolick!

[*Puts on her maſk.*

Enter Kitchen.

Kitchen. Your ſervant, madam!

Lett. Your ſervant, good Sir!

[*Pulling off her maſk.*

Kitchen. What! is it you, Mrs. Lettice? I thought it had been miſs Charlotte.

Lett. No, Sir; my miſtreſs could not poſſibly come herſelf—And ſo ſhe has ſent me in her place.

Kitchen. I am obliged to you for coming; but I have been ſworn at Highgate, Mrs. Lettice, and never take the maid inſtead of the miſtreſs.

Lett. But I ſuppoſe you have no objection to take the maid in order to get at the miſtreſs?

Kitchen. No, no! But what's the meaning of all this? How came you here in that habit?

Lett.

Lett. I'll tell you, Sir. Mrs. Crofs, you know, is as much fet againft you, as my mafter is your friend—And my young lady has a fad time with them both together, poor foul!

Kitchen. So fhe has, and yet fhe manages them pretty well too. She mixes with them as kindly as an egg between oil and vinegar.

Lett. Why, fhe muft feem to oblige my old lady; but her inclinations are entirely with you and her papa.

Kitchen. Yes, yes, I know that, Lettice.

Lett. But to make fhort of my ftory, Sir; her mama having unluckily difcovered that Mifs Charlotte had promifed to meet you in this habit, infifts on my putting it on, dreffes her daughter in a pink domino, and fends her to meet Mr. Marcourt.

Kitchen. The devil!

Lett. Patience, Sir; my young lady has turned all this to your advantage.

Kitchen. By what means?

Lett. She has contrived to make Mr. Marcourt imagine he is impofed upon. Her little fifter, who is as fharp as a needle, has been fet to tell him, that Mifs Charlotte ftill intends to meet you in this habit. This puts him upon a falfe train— fends him in purfuit of me—and in the mean
while

while you are to give my miſtreſs the meeting near the great booth, Sir.

Kitchen. Excellent! I'll away this very inſtant.

Lett. Stay, ſir. As I live, yonder comes Mr. Marcourt. If he ſees you leave me ſo abruptly, he will hardly take me for my young miſtreſs. Suppoſe you ſeem to have me under your care, and wait a few moments for a favourable opportunity to ſlip off to your appointment.

Kitchen. I'll do it.

Lett. He's juſt here. I muſt on with my maſk, and not open my lips, for fear of diſcovery.

[*Puts on her maſk.*

Enter Marcourt.

Marc. There they are, egad—juſt as the little girl told me—Your ſervant, ma'am.   [*Lettice curtſies.* Your ſervant, Mr. Kitchen!

Kitchen. Your humble ſervant, Sir!

Marc. Give me leave, Sir, to pay my reſpects to that lady.

Kitchen. Excuſe me, Sir. This lady has nothing to ſay to you.

Marc. You are miſtaken, Sir. I came on purpoſe to meet her.

Kitchen. That cannot be, Sir—This is an acquaintance of mine—and not the lady you mean.

Marc.

Marc. But I am convinced it is, Sir.

Kitchen. Pho! prithee, man! A lady in a mask is like a dish under cover; you can never tell what it is.

Marc. Pardon me, Sir. This may be disguised in the dressing; but I like the dish, and must taste of it.   [*Taking hold of Lettice.*

Kitchen. Let the lady alone, Sir!

Marc. This way, madam!

Kitchen. Zounds, Mr. Marcourt!

   [*Marcourt struggles with Lettice—she screams.*

Enter Cross and Mrs. Cross.

Cross. Hey-day! What is all this?

Kitchen. Only Mr. Marcourt, Sir, that will fall on without invitation. Here's a lady complains of his rudeness.

Cross. Rudeness! in my house! for shame, Mr. Marcourt!—This is your man of quality, Mrs. Cross.

Marc. Only a masquerade frolick; nothing else, Sir.

Cross. Well then—by the laws of all masquerades, the mask being taken off puts an end to impertinence—Pull off your mask, and put him to the blush, madam.

Kitchen. By no means, Sir.

Cross.

Crofs. Why not ? She fhall pull it off, and teach him how to behave himfelf.

Mrs. Crofs. No, no ; the lady muft not pull her mafk off.

Crofs. But I fay, fhe fhall.

Mrs. Crofs. But I fay, fhe fhall not.

Crofs. But fhe fhall, Mrs. Crofs.

Mrs. Crofs. But fhe fhall not, Mr. Crofs.

Marc. Ay, fay, let the lady unmafk, and I'll be fatisfied.

Mrs. Crofs. What ! are you mad, Mr. Marcourt?

Marc. My dear Mrs. Crofs, you are not in the fecret !   [*takes hold of Lettice.*

Lett. No violence, I befeech you, Sir ! the fight is not worth fo much importunity.   [*unmafks.*

Marc. Confufion !—Lettice ?

Lett. At your fervice, Sir !   [*curtfies.*

Crofs. Lettice ! in that habit ? Where is my daughter ?

Mrs. Crofs. I knew fhe was not here—Don't be uneafy, my dear ! I underftood Mr. Kitchen was defirous of a rendezvous ; fo I put the change upon him, thinking Lettice a more proper companion for him than my daughter. Ha, ha, ha !

Crofs. Death and the devil ! Am I deceived then ? fooled by my wife too!

                                        Kitchen.

Kitchen. Have patience, Sir. Many things happen between the cup and the lip. Sweet meat may have four fauce, they fay. A word with you. [*Talks apart with Crofs, while Mrs. Crofs converfes with Marcourt.*

Mrs. Crofs. But where is the girl all this while, Mr. Marcourt?

Marc. Devil fetch me, if I know, madam. I took Lettice for her.

Mrs. Crofs. What! were you deceived too? How could you poffibly be fo abfurd? Did not I agree to put Lettice into the Turkifh habit, and to drefs Charlotte in the pink domino?

[*Kitchen goes out here.*

Marc. Yes—but I was told I was impofed upon—and now I, begin to think I have made a fool of myfelf.

Mrs. Crofs. I drefs'd Charlotte, and left her in my room waiting for you.—I never knew any thing fo ridiculous! However, there can be no great harm done—it is plain fhe is not with Mr. Kitchen, you fee.

Crofs. [*Overhearing.*] Don't be too fure of that, Mrs. Crofs! Mr. Marcourt and you are but weak politicians. You fettle your own plan of operations, and never confider the motions of the enemy.

Mrs.

Mrs. Crofs. What motions! Where's Mr. Kitchen? gone?

Crofs. Yes—gone. Gone to marry my daughter. Mr. Marcourt rather chofe to make up to Lettice, you fee.

Mrs. Crofs. If fhe marries Mr. Kitchen, I'll never fee her face again.—To have your way in every thing! I cannot bear it!

Crofs. Rave on, my dear! We muft give lofers leave to talk, you know. Let them laugh that win!

Mrs. Crofs. Provoking infolence! I fhall die with vexation.

Crofs. Ha, ha, ha! poor woman!

Enter Fleece.

Crofs. Mr. Fleece! how do you, Sir? I am glad to fee you—heartily glad to fee you, Mr. Fleece.

Mrs. Crofs. How do you do, Mr. Fleece?

Fleece. Very well, I thank you, ma'am. I wifh you joy, ma'am—I wifh you joy of Mifs Charlotte's marriage, Mr. Crofs.

Crofs. My daughter's marriage!—Look you there, ma'am.—Tol derol, lol derol, lol—She's married, you fay?

Fleece. Yes, Sir; I left the couple at the church-door.

Crofs. Tol derol, lol derol, lol!

Mrs. Crofs. Charlotte married! to whom? to Mr. Kitchen, Mr. Fleece?

Crofs. Mr. Kitchen! ay, to be fure—whom fhould it be elfe, Mrs. Crofs?

Fleece. Mr. Kitchen! lackaday, no, ma'am—not Mr. Kitchen, Sir; I never heard of the gentle-man.

Marc. Well faid, my little woolcomber!—nor any body elfe, I believe.

Mrs. Crofs. Not Mr. Kitchen. Mind that, Mr. Crofs!

Crofs. Not Mr. Kitchen? Why then, who the devil is fhe married to?

Fleece. To Colonel Frankly, Sir.

Marc. Colonel Frankly! there's a fly dog now!

Mrs. Crofs. Well—I don't care who it is, fo as it is not Mr. Kitchen.

Marc. I am infinitely obliged to you, ma'am.

Crofs. 'Sdeath, Sir! but I'll fet all Stratford in a blaze. Did not you receive a letter from us about this affair?

Fleece.

Fleece. I did, Sir, from Mifs Charlotte—and fubfcribed with your's and Mrs. Crofs's approbation.—I obeyed your orders precifely, took this houfe immediately, and had the banns afked between the parties.

Crofs. Well! and the parties were my daughter and Mr. Kitchen.

Mrs. Crofs. No; my daughter and Mr. Marcourt.

Fleece. Neither; but your daughter and Colonel Frankly. Here are my credentials, Sir—the letter in your's, Mrs. Crofs's, and Mifs Charlotte's, handwriting. [*Delivers the letter.*

Crofs. So, fo! the little gipfy has deceived us both then.—She told me fhe would put in Mr. Kitchen's name.

Mrs. Crofs. And me, that fhe would deceive you, and infert Mr. Marcourt's.

Marc. Inftead of which, fhe has put in Colonel Frankly's—A bubble, by Jupiter!—My wager with Kitchen is a drawn bet then.

Enter Kitchen.

Marc. Ha! my brother in adverfity, where do you come from?

Kitchen. From church.—I arrived juft at the conclufion of the ceremony; but the latter end of

U 2   a feaft

a feaſt is better than the beginning of a fray, they ſay. We ſhall have a Jubilee wedding of it. There is the bride and bridegroom, with all Stratford, at my heels.

Mrs. Croſs. They ſha'n't enter my doors. I won't ſee their faces.

Kitchen. You had better, madam; or this affair will make us all very ridiculous.

Mrs. Croſs. Don't tell me—to be treated in ſuch a ſhameful manner! I will have nothing to ſay to them—and if Mr. Croſs has a grain of ſpirit, he will turn the undutiful wretch out of doors, and cut her off with a ſhilling.

Croſs. But I ſhall do no ſuch thing, Mrs. Croſs. My conduct ſhall be juſt the reverſe, madam. I will receive them with open arms: For if any thing has been amiſs, it has been entirely your fault.

Mrs. Croſs. My fault! how can that be?

Croſs. Very eaſily. If you had been of my mind, and had not encouraged the girl to be diſobedient, ſhe would not have been undutiful.

Mrs. Croſs. Well—and if you had been of my mind, would not it have been juſt the ſame thing?

Croſs. I begin to think we have both been to blame.

Enter

Enter Charlotte and Colonel Frankly.

Frankly. Permit us, Sir, to throw ourfelves at your feet, and to hope for your's and Mrs. Crofs's forgivenefs. My Charlotte thought it impoffible to prevail on both to confent to the fame match, and that is her only excufe for marrying without the approbation of either.

Crofs. Your apology is a fevere reproof, Sir.

Mrs. Crofs. I don't care—fo fhe is not wife to Mr. Kitchen.

Kitchen. Faith, madam, it gives me no uneafinefs. I have been roafted a little, it is true—but not fo much as my friend here.—He got into the wheel, and turned himfelf.

Marc. No matter—I fcorn to be outdone in good humour—and as this marriage has begun in mafquerade, if the prefent good company will adjourn to the Jubilee-mafked-ball this evening, I will moft chearfully attend them there.

Mrs. Crofs. Oh, as to the mafquerade, it is a genteel affair, and I like it of all things.

Crofs. Come then, Mrs. Crofs! It was impoffible we both fhould have been pleafed; fo let us not repine that Charlotte has fatisfied neither. We may, however, derive from this incident one material piece of inftruction—That no family can be

well

well governed, where there is a difagreement between thofe who are placed at the head of it—
and that nothing is fo neceffary as harmony among
thofe whofe interefts are fo intimately connected
as thofe of Man and Wife.

END of the SECOND VOLUME.

www.ingramcontent.com/pod-product-compliance
Lightning Source LLC
Chambersburg PA
CBHW020845020726
47497CB00005B/1269